Karen looked up at him. "Penny for your thoughts."

"I was just thinking about you. Us. How much I'm enjoying your company."

She smiled. "You're not so bad yourself."

Damian reached up and stroked a finger down her cheek and lowered his head. He hovered close enough for their breath to mingle, waiting, seeking permission. She hesitated for a brief moment, then tilted her head upward. He touched his mouth to hers, once, twice. Her lips parted beneath his, and he slid his tongue inside. He hadn't kissed a woman like this in a while—five years to be exact—but it didn't take long for him to catch up. She tangled her tongue with his, and he groaned deep in his throat. He turned, leaned against the rail, widened his stance and pulled her between his legs.

Karen wrapped her arms around his neck, grabbed the back of his head and held him in place. Damian had no problem with that. He had no intention of letting go—not until he got his fill, which in his estimation might take all night. He angled his head and deepened the kiss.

Dear Reader,

You met Karen Morris in *Just to Be with You* as Janae's outspoken best friend. Having suffered one heartbreak too many, she vows to stay away from men. But when Damian Bradshaw comes to her rescue, her vow takes a flying leap.

Widowed at a young age, Damian can't imagine falling in love again. His character grew out of witnessing someone very close to me go through a similar experience but eventually find love again. It was a joy to watch Damian's heart warm to love a second time. With her alluring personality and passion for life, Karen is his perfect match. Though she's hesitant, he's determined to make her his. It doesn't hurt that the chemistry between them sizzles!

I hope you enjoy Karen and Damian's journey to love.

Visit me at www.sheryllister.com or Facebook (Author Sheryl Lister) to find out what I'm working on next.

Blessings,

Sheryl

All of Me

SHERYL LISTER

HARLEQUIN® KIMANI™ ROMANCE

Recycling programs
for this product may
not exist in your area.

ISBN-13: 978-0-373-86387-7

All of Me

H HARLEQUIN®

Printed in U.S.A.

™ www.Harlequin.com

Sheryl Lister has enjoyed reading and writing for as long as she can remember. When she's not reading, writing or playing chauffeur, Sheryl can be found on a date with her husband or in the kitchen creating appetizers and bite-size desserts. She holds a BS in occupational therapy and a post-professional MS in occupational therapy from San Jose State University. She resides in California and is a wife, mother of three and pediatric occupational therapist.

Books by Sheryl Lister

Harlequin Kimani Romance

Just to Be with You
All of Me

Visit the Author Profile page at
Harlequin.com for more titles

For Brandi

Acknowledgments

To my Heavenly Father, thank You for Your love, mercy and grace.

To my real-life hero, Lance Lister, I'll love you to the end of time.

To my girls, family and friends, thank you for your love and unwavering support.

A special thank-you to Sharon Blount and Building Relationships Around Books book club. Thank you for your support and encouragement. You rock!

Chapter 1

Karen Morris stood off to the side in the Sapphire Room, one of the cruise ship's private dining rooms, smiling as her best friend approached. "Girl, you look so beautiful." Janae Simms had just exchanged wedding vows with popular R & B artist and producer Terrence "Monte" Campbell.

Janae smoothed a hand over the bodice of her white chiffon strapless A-line gown with a beaded motif accent at the hip. "Thanks."

"So, how does it feel to be a married woman?"

"I never thought I'd be this happy."

"Yeah. If that smile gets any wider, you'll be competing with the sun."

Janae giggled and looped her arm in Karen's. "I'm so glad you're my friend."

"Me, too."

"Come on. You need to help me eat some of my cake. We'll have a chance to talk more over lunch Monday."

"Lunch? Aren't you and Terrence going to be a little busy this week?"

Janae smiled and wiggled her eyebrows. "We'll be plenty busy, but he has to rehearse for his show that's on Wednesday night." He was one of several performers on the weeklong jazz cruise. "So, are we on for lunch?"

"Definitely."

After she ate a small piece of cake, Janae's brother Devin asked Karen to dance. Then she enjoyed dances with Janae's other two brothers and father. She started toward her table only to be pulled back to the floor by Donovan Wright, Terrence's best man and manager. By the time the short affair concluded, her feet were killing her.

Janae came up behind her. "Karen, we're leaving now. What time do you want to meet on Monday?"

She grinned and glanced over to where Terrence stood watching them. "Maybe you should be the one to decide. Your new husband looks like he's ready to eat you up."

"The feeling is mutual. How about one o'clock?"

"That'll work. I'll meet you at the entrance to the buffet." They spent another minute talking and then Karen said, "Enjoy your wedding night."

"I plan to," Janae said with a wink.

Karen smiled and shook her head, recalling how the two had met. She had practically dragged Janae to Terrence's—or Monte, as he was known in the music world—concert. What started as a backstage meet and greet after the concert had ended in marital bliss for her friend. She briefly wondered if she would get her own fairy-tale ending, then shoved the thought aside. *The only thing I'm focusing on is having a good time for the next week. Good music, good food, fabulous islands...me time.*

Janae's parents and Terrence's grandparents had elected not to cruise, so Karen stayed behind with Janae's brothers to see them off. She followed the family back down the hallway leading to the ship's entrance, where they would disembark. As they said their goodbyes, male laughter drew her attention.

She turned to see three men standing nearby, engaged in a lively conversation. All three were good-looking, but one in particular piqued her interest. He stood a few inches taller than his companions, with broad shoulders and the muscular build of a professional athlete. Her gaze lingered over his smooth golden brown features—close-cropped dark hair, chiseled jaw and full lips curved in a slight smile. The man was a serious piece of eye candy. Her gaze traveled over his body, then back up to his face to find him watching her with quiet intensity. Her heart rate kicked up a notch. Embarrassed that he had caught her staring, she quickly turned away. Moments later, she couldn't resist another peek.

Suddenly, he paused with the drink halfway to his lips and swung his head in her direction. His smile inched up, and he saluted her with his drink. Her breath stalled in her lungs.

"Karen?"

"Huh, what?" She tore her gaze away and tried to focus on what Janae's mother was saying. "I'm sorry. What did you say, Mrs. Simms?"

She chuckled. "I asked if you were going to miss your students this week."

"I love my little darlings, but I plan to enjoy a week without lesson plans and mediating 'he said, she said' arguments."

After a few minutes of polite conversation and a round of hugs, Karen wound her way around the ship toward her suite. Several men called out greetings and offered to buy her a drink, and one propositioned her for more, but she ignored them all. A vision of Mr. Eye Candy worked its way into her mind and she pushed it away, reminding herself that she was taking a break from men and focusing on herself and her career goals.

Damian Bradshaw half listened to his friends as they once again listed all the reasons why this cruise was a good idea. The cruise was an annual event, and they had invited him several times over the years, but he always declined. Troy Ellis slung an arm around his shoulders. "Man, you can't tell me you're not looking forward to some fun aboard a luxury cruise. Good music, good food, exotic ports—"

"And a ship full of fine, single women," Kyle Jamison cut in. "Mmm, mmm, mmm," he said, staring after a group of women walking by and smiling at them. "See what I mean? Damian, this is exactly what you need to get back in the groove."

"Who says I want to get back in the groove?" Damian muttered.

Troy dropped his arm and shook his head. "It's been five years, Damian. When do you think you'll be ready to move on?"

Damian clenched his jaw. He didn't need to be reminded how long it had been since he lost his wife. He had lived every one of those moments without her, counted every second since she'd died from a freak accident. He had no desire to open his heart to the possibility of pain again. "I have moved on."

Kyle crossed his arms and pinned Damian with a glare. "Have you really? You're one step up from a recluse. You're either at the office, at the gym or locked in your house. You probably don't even remember how to date."

"We have a lot to do at the office," Damian countered. The three friends co-owned a consulting firm and traveled around the country providing safety training to schools and corporate groups.

"All of which our dynamic office assistant, Delores, can handle until we get back. He's right, Damian," Troy said softly. "It's time. Joyce wouldn't want you to live the rest of your life alone." He grinned. "And, since we know you've been out of the game for a while, we'll be more than happy to offer you some pointers on how to attract a woman," he added, trying to lighten the mood.

Damian chuckled. "Yeah, I bet."

"We need to get this party started right. I'm going to get a drink," Kyle said.

Troy nodded. "Good idea. Let's go."

"I'll wait for you guys."

"You want me to bring you something?" Troy asked.

"Yeah. Bring me a beer." He watched them saunter off and flirt with two passing women.

He leaned against the railing, shoved his hands into his pockets and contemplated his friends' words. He hated to admit it, but they were right. He'd immersed himself in his job, staying at the office way past normal hours, working out at the gym to the point of exhaustion, then going home to an empty house and losing himself in thoughts of what could have been, what should have been. Damian rarely did anything that could be considered fun and hadn't thought about taking a trip. Even when Joyce was alive, she preferred a quiet evening at home to going out or leaving town, so they'd never traveled far. When they did, they only went on occasional weekend getaways.

He took in his surroundings. Boarding passengers streamed past him, their animated chatter and excitement filling the air. He couldn't remember the last time he had taken a real vacation. Maybe he needed this cruise after all.

"Here you go."

He accepted the beer from Troy. "Thanks."

Kyle held up his bottle. "I'd like to propose a toast. To a week of great music and endless pleasures."

"Hear, hear!" Troy said.

They looked at Damian expectantly. Sighing, he clinked his bottle against theirs, then tilted it to his lips.

Kyle smiled. "Now, the first lesson when picking up women is to find one who wants no attachments beyond the week and is just out for a good time."

"Usually, she'll be with a group of women, make eye contact and check you out from head to toe," Troy added.

Kyle nodded. "She'll find a way to cross your path at least twice, be wearing an enticing little number and give you a smile that says she's up for whatever you want."

"If you're interested, return her smile but don't approach her right away." Troy leaned closer. "Continue to flirt from a distance, maybe send her a drink. You know, heighten the desire."

"Now you're ready to make your move," Kyle said, clapping Damian on the shoulder.

"And, because we knew you wouldn't, we slipped a couple boxes of condoms into your bag," Troy finished with a smug smile. "Think about it, this'll be the perfect way to make that first step back into the land of the living."

"I'm thirty-three years old. I don't need you to tell me how to approach a woman," Damian gritted out. Kyle and Troy laughed. "What?"

"Man, you've been out of the game so long you wouldn't know what to say, even if she held up a sign saying 'Unattached and Available.'" Kyle paused thoughtfully. "Actually, you never really dated at all, since you and Joyce sort of hooked up in college."

He skewered Kyle with a look.

"You know I'm right. Yeah, you dated a few women back then—and I use the term *dated* loosely—but you and Joyce always circled back to each other."

Rather than responding and risk knocking Kyle out, he took another swig of his beer.

"Lay off Damian, Kyle. Give the brother a chance. We've only been on the boat for forty-five minutes, and we haven't even left the dock yet."

"Yeah. Lay off. I'm perfectly capable of deciding whether I want a woman or not." Though he mostly subscribed to the "or not" category. He had gone out a few times since his wife's death, but never progressed past a couple of dates and a few chaste kisses.

Kyle gave him a sidelong glance. "You sure? Because I can't have you embarrassing me and ruining my reputation with some lame pickup lines."

Damian shook his head and laughed, giving in to Kyle's wack sense of humor. "Man, I don't know how we've been friends all these years."

"Hell, you need somebody to keep you straight. Leaving you to your own devices, we might find you living as a monk with no sense of humor." They all laughed.

"Whatever."

Out of his periphery, he noticed a woman staring his way. She was standing in a group with two older couples, a younger couple and two other men. Their eyes locked, and he felt a kick in the gut. An embarrassed expression crossed her face, and she turned away. He willed her to look his way again, wanting to know if he'd imagined the spark of awareness. When she finally glanced back, he felt it again. A slow grin made its way over his face, and he saluted her with his bottle.

"Earth to Damian." Troy waved his hand in front of Damian's face.

Damian jerked back. "What?"

"Are you listening? What are you looking at?"

"Nothing," he murmured. He idly sipped his drink while scanning the woman from head to toe. She had flawless mocha skin and a strikingly beautiful face. The strapless gray dress she wore clung subtly to her lush curves and gave way to long, toned legs and stirred a desire he had never experienced, or at least hadn't experienced in a long time. He frowned, not liking the direction of his thoughts.

"Whoa. Hold up. I *know* you're not staring at the woman in the gray dress," Kyle said. "Didn't you hear anything I just said?" He shook his head. "Nah, bro, don't even go there. Nothing about her says 'I just want a good time.'

She has *permanent* and *keeper* stamped all over her. She's standing with old people, for goodness' sake!"

Damian ignored Kyle and continued to observe the woman as she hugged the older couples and then weaved her way through the crowd. A few men tried to stop her, but she shook her head and kept walking. One man couldn't seem to take no for an answer and reached out to grab her. He handed his bottle to Troy.

"I'll be right back." He moved with determined strides toward the woman.

As Damian approached, he heard the man say, "Hey, beautiful. How about you keep me company this week? I promise to show you a good time."

Clearly he'd had too much to drink if his slurred voice was any indication.

"No, thanks." She gasped sharply when the man grabbed her around the waist and pulled her to him.

"Aw, come on."

A scowl settled on her beautiful face. "You have about one second to remove your arm or—"

"You heard the lady," Damian interrupted. "I'm sure you don't want your cruise to end before the boat leaves the dock." The man spun around and opened his mouth to speak, but obviously thought better of it. Damian towered over the man by a good six inches and outweighed him by forty pounds of pure muscle.

The man dropped his arm, muttered something about stuck-up women and took off down the corridor.

Damian glanced at the woman who barely reached his shoulder in her heels. "Are you okay?"

"I… Yes. Thank you. Although I could have handled it."

He chuckled in faint amusement. "I have no doubt about that. Would you like an escort to your room, or will you be all right?"

"I'll be fine. Thanks again."

"My pleasure. Perhaps I'll see you again."

"Perhaps."

Damian followed the sway of her hips until she was out of sight, then made his way back over to where his friends waited.

"Please don't tell me you made a move on that woman," Kyle lit into Damian as soon as he returned.

"Give it a rest, Kyle. I saw a guy harassing her and just made sure she was okay. I didn't even get her name."

"What do you mean you didn't get her name? Man, you're more out of practice than I thought," Troy said with a laugh.

Damian rolled his eyes. "Shut up, Troy. Like I said before, I don't know why I still keep you guys around. I have plenty of time to find out her name...if I want to."

Troy's eyebrows shot up. "Sounds like you're interested."

He glanced over his shoulder in the direction she had gone, then faced his friends. "Maybe." Up close, she was even more beautiful, and damn if he wasn't attracted to her. As Kyle noted, everything about her shouted *relationship*, not *fling*. But he wasn't looking for either, or was he? At any rate, things were starting to look up. Coming on this cruise might not have been such a bad idea after all, especially if he got a chance to spend a little time with his mystery lady. Yep, things were definitely looking up.

Karen felt the heat of her rescuer's gaze on her back, but she refused to turn around. The man was positively scrumptious with a rich, deep voice that poured over her like warm melted chocolate. From a distance she hadn't been able to discern the color of his eyes, but with him standing so near, she could see the green flecks in his light brown eyes—eyes that reflected friendliness and something else she couldn't identify. He didn't seem like the usual guy on the prowl. She shook her head to clear her thoughts. Why did she even care? She didn't.

Or at least, that was what she told herself.

Chapter 2

Karen entered her cabin, locked the door, dropped down in the closest chair and kicked off her shoes. If she didn't care, why was her heart beating faster? And why did the prospect of seeing him again send a shiver of excitement down her spine? She pushed off the chair and went to change into more comfortable clothing to get ready for the muster drill.

She searched for him at the drill and during dinner, and experienced a twinge of disappointment at not seeing him. Devin and Donovan had invited her to hang out with them for the evening listening to a couple of performances. She particularly enjoyed the performance by Eric Darius. The young saxophonist had a way of infusing jazz and funk that had everyone in the room on their feet dancing, including her. By the time she made it to her room that evening, Karen was beyond exhausted. Rather than take Friday off, she had worked the full day and then taken an overnight flight to Florida. She slept as much as she could on the plane and had taken a short nap this afternoon, but the lack of sleep had taken its toll. She showered and brushed her teeth within fifteen minutes and crawled into bed. The lulling movement of the ship relaxed her, and she drifted off to sleep quickly.

When she woke up the next morning, Karen felt no more rested than she had the night before. Images of a sexy stranger had kept her tossing and turning all night.

Instead of going to the dining room for breakfast, she opted for a muffin and coffee from room service. After dressing, she went out on the balcony. Miles and miles of deep blue water stretched out before her, and a slight breeze blew across her face.

She would have to thank Terrence again for the suite. He insisted on paying for her room as a thank-you for bringing Janae to the concert that night. She smiled, thinking about how reluctant Janae had been about dating a superstar, but Terrence had proven himself more than worthy of her love and devotion.

Although happy for her friend, she couldn't stop the pang of sadness that hit her. Automatically, Karen's thoughts shifted to her spineless, cheating ex-boyfriend. One minute they had been looking at wedding rings, and the next she was reclaiming her single status. She'd given him her love and almost two years of her life, but obviously, it hadn't meant anything. The old pain and anger rose to the surface, and she drew in a deep breath. She had given Andre Robertson enough of her time and energy and didn't intend to waste another second on his trifling behind. She glanced out over the water once more before going inside.

Today was a new day, and she looked forward to all the activities and concerts. And, despite the lecture she had given herself about not getting involved with another man, she couldn't help hoping she crossed paths with the gorgeous hunk again.

Grabbing her book and sunglasses, Karen left her room. She meandered around the ship for a while, then went out to the deck. She found an empty spot at the railing and braced her forearms on the dark, polished wood. This trip was exactly what she needed to clear her mind. She stood there a few minutes longer and noticed someone vacate a lounger near the pool. She quickly claimed it. Pushing her sunglasses higher up on her nose, she leaned back, closed her eyes and took a deep, cleansing breath. Opening her eyes again, she stared up at the cloudless blue sky and smiled. The sun shone and warmed her skin, funky jazz blared from speakers and people all around her danced and laughed. She felt the stress melt from her body as she picked up her book.

Karen was so engrossed in the characters that she jumped when a hand touched her shoulder. Her head snapped up. A man stood next to her wearing swim trunks and holding a drink in his hand. She guessed him to be in his late fifties. He had on an ill-fitting toupee and really should have put on a shirt.

"You look like you could use some company," he said, leering at her with a gap-toothed smile that made her skin crawl.

Keeping her features neutral and trying not to cringe, she said, "I'm just fine reading my book *alone*."

He continued as if she hadn't spoken. "I think we could have a good time together. I'd be remiss in my duties as a man to let a beautiful woman like you sit here all alone."

She barely stifled an eye roll. "Thanks for your concern, but I'd like to get back to my book." She picked up the book and started reading, hoping he would get the hint and move on.

Finally, he walked away. *Good grief. I must be attracting every loser on this ship!* First the man in the hallway, now this guy. She took a discreet glance around to make sure he was gone. When she didn't see him, Karen sighed in relief and shook her head. She turned back, and her gaze collided with the man who had invaded her dreams. He stood in the pool staring at her, his hazel eyes twinkling with amusement. The corners of his mouth kicked up into a sexy smile, and her pulse spiked. Someone bumped him and he looked away, breaking the connection. She shook herself and turned her attention back to the book.

After reading the same page three times, Karen gave up all pretense of trying to read. Her eyes strayed back to the pool and searched until she spotted him again. Hidden behind her shades, she studied his broad shoulders, his sculpted chest and arms and the strong lines of his handsome face. He started across the pool, and she was fascinated with his powerful strokes and by the play of muscles in his back as he swam. *Have mercy!* She stared until he disappeared from her vision. Dropping her head, she once again tried to concentrate on her novel.

She had finally managed to get back into the story when a shadow fell over her. She immediately thought Mr. Toupee had returned but went still when she heard the low, sexy voice.

"I see you're still fighting off the masses."

Karen's head popped up. It was *him*. Her mouth went dry. Rivulets of water ran down his golden chest and sculpted abs before disappearing beneath his black trunks. The wet trunks clung to muscled thighs and drew her attention to the impressive bulge resting at his groin. He wiped at his face with a towel, glanced down and chuckled, bringing her out of her lustful thoughts. Gathering herself, she said, "Um, something like that." His heated gaze burned a slow path from her face, lingered at her breasts and continued down to her exposed legs and back up. Her breath caught.

"Maybe you should find yourself a bodyguard."

"Are you applying for the position?" she asked flirtatiously.

His brow lifted. Before he could answer, one of the men she had seen him with yesterday called out to him. He held up a hand, signaling for them to wait, then turned back to her and angled his head thoughtfully. "You never know."

"Hmm, interesting."

"You have no idea." Blessing her with another heart-stopping smile, he said, "I'll see you around."

"That man is too fine," she mumbled to herself as he sauntered off. Karen had no idea what had gotten into her, flirting with him like that. But she couldn't help herself. Something about the man fascinated her. She had always been bold by nature, and when she was growing up, her mouth had gotten her into trouble more times than she could count. Her mother often said, *Karen, one of these days your mouth is going to write a check your butt can't cash!* She wondered if this might be one of those times.

Damian was still chuckling when he reached Troy and Kyle. He couldn't remember the last time he'd flirted with a woman, but their verbal play stimulated him and filled him with newfound energy. A bodyguard? He'd be more than happy to guard every inch of her sexy body.

"Damian, didn't we have this discussion yesterday? You need to find a woman who just wants a one-night stand. Don't waste your time. She's not interested," Kyle said.

"She's not interested? How do you know she's not interested?" She had seemed to enjoy their exchange as much as he did.

Kyle threw his hands up in exasperation. "Trust me, she's not. Remember—relationship, permanent, keeper? *Not* a cruise-week hookup."

"Kyle, you haven't even spoken to the woman." Damian turned to Troy. "I guess you have something to say, too?"

Troy held up his hands in surrender. "Hey, I've decided that you're a lost cause. You've smiled more in the last twenty-four hours since meeting her than you have in the last twenty-four months. Any woman who can draw you out of your funk that fast…I say go for it."

He shot a glare at Kyle, then clapped Troy on the shoulder. "Thanks."

Kyle folded his arms across his chest. "Don't say I didn't warn you."

"Your warning is duly noted," Damian drawled. "I'm going to shower. I'll meet you guys at the grill in half an hour," he called over his shoulder as he headed for his room.

Once there, he stripped, turned on the shower and stood under the warm stream. While he was washing, his thoughts wandered back to the woman on the deck. Yeah, she did make him smile, and laugh, too. He frowned. He hadn't even thought to ask her name. Again. "I've really been out of the game a long time," he muttered, shaking his head. *Next time,* he promised himself.

Karen woke up Monday morning, read over the list of ship activities and found a morning Zumba class. She didn't make it to the gym as often as she liked, but so far, things were still holding firm. Since she planned to enjoy herself over the week, she figured she might as well offset some of those calories by taking the exercise class. She arrived on the crowded deck just as the class began, found a spot near the edge and jumped into the routine. Halfway through the session, she had second thoughts about her choice. The muscles in every part of her body burned, and she could barely catch her breath.

"Lord, have mercy! I don't know what I was thinking, interrupting my sleep for this torture session," the woman next to her said, breathing heavily. "You can best believe I'm not doing it again. I'm gonna need an extra cocktail later on to make up for this."

Karen let out a tired laugh. "I hear you."

When class ended, Karen trudged back to her room and collapsed on the bed with a loud groan. Knowing she needed to shower, she lay there awhile longer, then dragged herself up and into the bathroom. In the shower, she let the hot water stream over her aching muscles until they loosened up. After washing up, she slipped on a robe and pulled out her novel.

When she glanced up and checked the time, she realized it was almost time to meet Janae. Karen discarded the robe and put on her red halter dress. She used the flat-iron to style her chin-length hair so that the strands fell in soft layers, framing her face. She told herself she wasn't taking extra care with her appearance just in case she ran into Mr. Eye Candy again, but she knew it was a lie. At the last minute, she slicked her lips with gloss, stepped into her jeweled sandals and left.

Janae was already waiting when she arrived.

"Girl, I can't believe you beat me here," Karen said. "Your sexy husband let you out of his sight?"

"Barely," she answered with a chuckle. "He told me the rehearsal wouldn't last more than a couple of hours and that he'd find me as soon as he finished."

"Well, let's not waste time. I'm starving, and I *know* you need to eat. Gotta keep up your strength." They burst out laughing and headed to the buffet.

There were so many offerings that Karen had a hard time choosing what to put on her plate. She settled on a mixed green salad, baked tilapia with lobster cream and smoked Gouda macaroni and cheese topped with panko bread crumbs. She placed the plate on a table, then went back for a drink.

"I see you got the tilapia, too," Janae said when she returned.

"That lobster cream smelled heavenly, and I couldn't resist." They ate in silence for a few minutes before Karen asked, "Do you miss San Jose and teaching?" Janae had taught a special education class at the same school where Karen taught, but she'd recently relocated to Los Angeles, where Terrence lived.

"Not too much. So far, I like LA. Some days I miss teaching, but Terrence turned one of the rooms in the house into an art studio, and I've been painting."

"Girl, those landscapes are breathtaking. I know you don't like the spotlight, but have you thought any more about a gallery showing?"

"You know me too well. Terrence has been great keeping the tabloids out of our business, so it hasn't been as bad as I thought. But, to answer your question, I have thought about it. I actually have an appointment with a gallery director when we get back—someone Terrence's grandmother knows."

Karen's eyes widened. "Oh, my goodness. Are you serious? That's fantastic. You know I'll be at your first show."

"She has to like the pieces first."

"Please. She's going to love them. I'm so happy for you." Karen's and Janae's family had been trying to convince Janae to pursue an art career for years.

Janae shrugged. "We'll see. Enough about me. What's going on? You mentioned something about Andre. I thought you guys broke up a few months ago."

She set her fork down on the plate and expelled a harsh breath. "We did. Before I left Friday, he called wanting to talk."

"Did you talk to him?"

"No. I let it go to voice mail. I don't have anything to say to him. He was the one who decided I wasn't good enough for him and sought out someone more to his liking, so…anyway, I've decided to put men on the back burner and focus all my attention on getting into administration. Hopefully, an opening will come up soon."

"You told me about that." Janae angled her head. "With all the programs you put in place last year for the fourth-grade team, I can see you as a school principal. Didn't you present district wide?"

She chuckled. "Yeah. But maybe I should start as an *assistant* principal or counselor first."

"You know, you can have a relationship and still pursue your goals."

"Look who's talking. If I remember correctly, you were the same way before you met Terrence. Weren't you always saying, 'I have my teaching and painting and that's enough'?"

Janae pointed her fork at Karen. "And *you* were the one telling me to get back out there and try again after Lawrence and Carter. Now I'm giving you back your own *good* advice." She waved a hand. "You're on a cruise ship with dozens of fine men, and I'm sure at least one of them will be more than happy to help you jump back into the saddle, so to speak."

Karen's mouth gaped. "What happened to shy little Janae? Being with Terrence has got you acting all wild."

Janae laughed. "Hey. What can I say? The man knows how to—"

Karen held up a hand. "Stop. I do not need to hear this. You know I've loved Monte his entire career, and it's hard enough not having lustful thoughts about him as it is without hearing details regarding his sexual prowess. The man is downright sexy."

"Actually, if I remember correctly, your description of him went something like rich milk chocolate skin, dark brown eyes, full, sexy lips framed by a goatee and over six feet of rock-hard muscle."

"I can't believe you remember that," she mumbled. "Anyway, now that you've ruined my fantasy, I'll just have to concentrate on work. Besides, I haven't met anyone who comes close to being that fine." As the words left her mouth, an image of the man she had met the first day popped into her mind, along with a strange sensation that had her heart pumping. She wondered if he was married.

He had been with two other men and she didn't see any women, but that didn't mean anything. What if he was single? Karen glanced around the room. With hundreds of people on the ship, she'd be lucky if she saw him again. Sighing softly, she resumed eating.

"There are plenty of handsome men roaming around here." Janae folded her arms. "As a matter of fact, I don't think you'll have a problem finding someone to spend time with."

Karen arched an eyebrow upon seeing the sly grin on Janae's face. "Really? And what makes you think that?"

"For one thing, I noticed several guys watching you when you were fixing your plate." A smile played around the corners of her mouth. She leaned forward and whispered, "For another, there's a positively gorgeous specimen of a man headed this way."

Karen whipped her head around, and her gaze collided with the man who had invaded her dreams for the past two nights. He looked good, wearing a pair of black linen shorts with a matching button-down shirt and black leather sandals. The muscles in her arms and calves were on prominent display, flexing with every movement. *Mouthwatering.* Her heart thudded in her chest as he came closer and stopped at their table.

"Good afternoon, ladies." He fixed his stare on Karen. "We meet again," her dream hunk said with a wink. "Any more problems?"

Janae leaned back in her chair and gave Karen a sidelong glance. A smile tugged at her lips.

Karen cut her a quick look, then said, "No. None."

"Glad to hear it." He stood there a moment longer, as if he wanted to say more. Finally, he stuck out his hand. "I don't think we've been properly introduced. I'm Damian."

She reached for his hand. "Karen." His large hand engulfed her smaller one. Warmth spread up her arm and through her body. She withdrew her hand and pulled her gaze from his. "This is my best friend, Janae."

He nodded politely and shook Janae's hand. "Hello."

"Nice to meet you, Damian."

"Well, I don't want to interrupt your lunch, but I just wanted to make sure Karen hadn't had any more trouble."

"Oh, you're not interrupting," Janae said. "Have a seat." She pushed back from the table and stood. "I'll be right back. I want to check out the dessert table."

Karen stifled a laugh when Janae mouthed, *Yummy*, behind his back. She looked up to where Damian still stood, seemingly waiting for an invitation to sit. She pointed to the empty chair next to her. "Please have a seat, Damian." *A strong name for a tall, strong-looking brother.*

He folded his body into the chair, and they both fell silent for a few moments.

He chuckled nervously. "It's been a while since I've been in the company of such a beautiful woman. I'm way out of practice and not real sure what to do anymore."

She laughed. "Well, no time like the present to find out."

He nodded. "So, are you traveling with a companion? I noticed the men you were with."

"If you're asking whether I'm single, the answer is yes, I am. Those were Janae's brothers. And you?"

"Same." He paused. "Would you like to join me for dinner this evening?"

"I'm sorry. I've already made plans."

His face fell.

"But I'm free tomorrow night."

A smile lit his face. "Marcus Johnson is performing tomorrow night. Would you like to go with me to the concert?"

Karen hesitated. She had planned to attend the show anyway and didn't want to go alone. But she was supposed to be taking a break from men, and in her head, she listed all the reasons why she should tell him no. However, something about Damian had captured her attention. Why not throw caution to the wind and have a little fun? Besides, after this week, she'd never see him again. "I'd love to."

He came to his feet. "Great."

"What time is the show?"

"It starts at eight, but I'll get there early to save us a seat."

"Sounds good. I'll meet you there."

"I'll be waiting. Enjoy the rest of your day, Karen." He pivoted and sauntered off.

"Okay." She slowly lowered her trembling hand to her lap and stared after him, remembering how good he looked from the back in those swim trunks—broad shoulders, tapered waist and tight, muscled butt. That sexy stroll had several women stopping to watch. She smiled. Tomorrow, he would be all hers.

"So I guess you won't be instituting that dating hiatus after all," Janae said, dropping into her chair.

"I might be willing to make an exception just for him," she said absently, still staring at Damian's retreating back.

"Wow. That must be a new record for the shortest dating hiatus ever."

Karen slowly turned her head and glared.

Janae checked her watch. "It lasted all of…four and a half minutes."

"Ha-ha. So you got jokes now." She tried to hold on to her scowl, but lost the battle when Janae started laughing. They laughed so hard, people at nearby tables turned to stare. When they were finally able to regain some semblance of calm, Karen said, "I haven't laughed that hard in a long time. I really miss hanging out with you."

"Yeah, so do I." Wiping tears of mirth from her eyes, Janae asked, "What did Damian mean by you having trouble? Did something happen?"

"Not really. On the way to my room after seeing your parents off, some drunk fool tried to grab me, talking about keeping him company for the cruise. I was two seconds from knocking him on his butt when Damian intervened. He even offered to walk me to my room. Then yesterday, he happened to be at the pool when another jerk tried to hit on me."

"Hmph. Fine and a gentleman. Are you guys going to meet up soon?"

She smiled and nodded. "We're going to Marcus Johnson's show tomorrow night."

"You go, girl. And if he turns out *not* to be a gentleman, we can toss him overboard."

They shared another laugh, remembering the time Karen had said the same thing about Terrence when he first showed an interest in Janae. But something told her that Damian was every bit the gentleman she thought him to be.

Damian couldn't keep the smile off his face as he left the dining room. Karen. He had thought about her all night but figured he probably wouldn't see her again so soon. He couldn't remember the last time he had anticipated going on a date so much. Excitement hummed in his veins, something no other woman in the past five years had been able to elicit. He made his way out to the deck, where an up-and-coming band was playing.

I wonder if she'll wear something like that red dress. He hoped so. The tasteful halter dress revealed the smooth skin of her back and shoulders, reminding him of whipped chocolate mousse. A vision of him trailing his hands and mouth along the expanse of her neck, shoulders and back flooded his mind, sending an unexpected jolt of lust to his groin, and shocking him in the process.

The parts of him he thought had died with his wife suddenly roared to life, followed by an immediate stab of guilt. His chest tightened. Damian threaded his way through the crowd crammed on the deck, moved to the railing and stared out over the water. His guilt was irrational, he knew, but he couldn't help following the flash of memories as they arose. The music and voices faded as his mind traveled back to Joyce.

He had taken her under his wing and helped her adjust to a new school after she moved in with her grandparents across from his house when they were fifteen. Her father's job had relocated to another state, and rather than uproot Joyce, her parents had allowed her to stay in North Carolina and finish high school. Their relationship had just sort of developed over time, and what started as friendship gave way to a gentle love ending in marriage. Pain settled in his chest. He would never forget the day he came home from work and found her unconscious at the bottom of the stairs. She had sustained a severe brain injury in the fall and died two days later.

He squeezed his eyes shut to block out the memories. He drew in a long breath and released it slowly. Damian repeated the process until the pressure in his chest eased. He had been grieving for five long years. Karen's face shimmered in his mind's eye. Joyce would always hold a place in his heart, but she was gone now. Maybe it was time for him to stop merely existing and actually start living. Someone bumped him, shattering his reverie. Slowly the music and voices came back into focus. People all around him clapped, danced and sang along with the band.

He glanced up to the sky, smiled softly and let the music seep into his soul. Today was a new day, a new beginning with a beautiful and intriguing woman in his future, and he planned to enjoy both.

Chapter 3

Karen and Janae had a little while longer to hang out before it was time for Janae to meet Terrence, so they sat in on a question-and-answer session with a jazz artist.

"Is Terrence doing a Q & A, too?"

"Yes. The show is Wednesday night, and he'll do the Q & A and autograph signing the following afternoon. Knowing Terrence, he'll probably sing a couple of songs, too. We're going to do a little sightseeing when we get to Nassau earlier in the day, then get back in time for the session."

"You guys aren't getting off in Grand Turks tomorrow and Jamaica on Wednesday?"

"No. He doesn't want to be too tired for the concert, so we'll hang out in the room. But he promised we'd take a trip to Jamaica soon."

Karen chuckled. "Locked in an exquisite suite aboard a luxury cruise with his new bride, yeah, I'm sure he'll be *well* rested."

"I'll go easy on him," Janae said with a laugh. "Are you coming?"

"Of course I'm coming to the show."

"Hmm. You might be otherwise preoccupied," she said with a smirk.

"I don't think so. If we happen to hit it off, he's welcome to join me, but I'm not missing that show. And you tell Terrence…well, Monte, I'd better get my autographed CD."

Janae laughed. "I'll make sure to pass the message along. It's really good."

"Wait. You've already heard it?" At Janae's grin, she frowned and folded her arms. "See, you just ain't right. I thought I was your BFF."

"You are. Gotta go find my hubby, before he comes looking for me." She gave a little wave and started off.

Karen stared with her mouth hanging open. "I am so going to get you, you little traitor!" she called after Janae. "You weren't even a big fan of his until I dragged you to that concert."

Janae just laughed and kept going.

Karen shook her head and headed for her own room.

Once the ship reached Grand Turks the following day, Karen disembarked only long enough to take a picture in front of the welcome sign and pick up a souvenir. Back in her room, she pulled out her novel and read on the balcony until it was time to leave for dinner. Knowing she wouldn't have time to change between dinner and the concert, she toyed with putting on something else.

Standing in front of the mirror, Karen glanced at her profile and decided against it. The turquoise halter dress was similar to the red one she'd worn the day before and made her look and feel sexy. She smoothed down her hair and touched up her makeup. Satisfied with her appearance, she picked up her small black leather cross-body purse with a braided jewel and leather strap and left.

Devin had insisted she have dinner with him and Donovan, so she wouldn't have to eat alone. Tonight, Janae's oldest brother and his wife, along with two of Terrence's other friends, joined them. During dinner, she laughed and conversed, but her thoughts were never far from Damian. Sure, the man gave new meaning to good-looking, but she hadn't come on this ship for some meaningless fling. Her goals were clear: see her best friend get married and refocus on her career. However, if that were truly the case, why had she agreed to meet him tonight? *Because I'm drawn to him in a way I can't explain.*

Nervousness took hold, and she took a huge gulp of her wine. By the time dinner concluded, she had downed two glasses, hoping they would calm the marbles rolling around in her belly. They didn't. She stood to excuse herself and had to endure Devin's inquisition. She used to think Janae was kidding about his overprotectiveness. Now she knew better. After assuring him she didn't need him to check out her date, Karen made a quick getaway.

A crowd had already gathered by the time Karen arrived at the theater. How in the world would she find Damian? She had no clue where to begin. She scanned the left side, squinting in the jam-packed space. Taking a step farther into the room, she leaned forward to see if he was sitting on one of the lower levels. A warm hand circled her waist, and she turned to give the offender a blistering retort, but froze when she heard the seductively familiar voice.

"Looking for someone?"

She turned slowly. Good grief. Every time she saw the man he looked better and better. Tonight he wore tailored dark trousers and a silk pullover that emphasized his well-defined arms, chest and abs. "Hey. I didn't see you." The heat from his body pressed against her ignited a slow burn. A shiver passed through her. She eased out of his embrace before she was tempted to do something crazy, like reach up and run her hands all over him to see if those muscles felt as firm as they looked. "Where are we sitting?"

Damian cupped her elbow and gently steered her to where he had seats saved near the front.

"Wow. How did you get such great seats?"

He chuckled softly. "It's our first date. I wanted to impress you, so I got here early."

First? The tone of his voice and the intensity of his gaze suggested there would be more than one date if he had anything to say about it. "Well, consider me impressed." The lounge had a mixture of theater chairs, semicircular booths for six or eight, tables with chairs and love seats for two. Of course, he had chosen the love seat. If it unnerved her how close he stood, she had no idea how she would manage to get through one or two hours with him sitting so near.

Damian gestured her to the seat, then sat next to her. He turned and reached for her hand. "Karen, I want to thank you for agreeing to come tonight." He lifted her hand to his lips and placed a soft kiss on the back.

Karen stifled a moan at the feeling of his warm lips against her skin and melted into the seat. "Um. Thank you for asking." She imagined those same lips trailing a path up her arm, over her shoulders…

Get it together, girl, an inner voice snapped, shattering the vision.

"And I'm *really* glad you have on another dress like that red one you were wearing yesterday. You look absolutely stunning."

"It's one of my favorites."

"Now it's one of mine."

Typically, she had no problem engaging in a little harmless flirtation with men, but Damian was messing with her equilibrium. Even with the lights low, she saw the fire in his eyes, and the flirty comeback poised on her tongue died a swift death. Earlier he had mentioned being out of practice with women. If he defined this as "out of practice," what would he be like *with* practice?

He leaned over to say something else, but before he could open his mouth, the lights went down in the theater, Marcus Johnson came up on the stage and the music began. *Thank goodness.* She needed a minute. If she had any doubts that he had more than a passing interest in her, the look in his eyes cleared it up. He was definitely interested. Just some casual fun, someone to pass the time with—that was what she told herself. She hadn't planned on this. She hadn't planned on *him*. And Lord help her, she was interested in him, too.

She glanced down at his long fingers tapping out the song's rhythm on his thigh. He had large hands, making her speculate about the size of certain other parts. Her pulse jumped. *Karen Lynette Morris, you stop it right now!* she chastised herself. *Get your mind out of the gutter.* Karen reached up and discreetly wiped the moisture gathering on her forehead. She needed to get a grip. She was sitting here fantasizing about a man she'd met two days ago, or actually yesterday. Whenever. The point was, she had no business thinking about him in those terms. She pushed the sensual thoughts to the back of her mind and focused on the music, letting the smooth piano jazz sounds take over.

Soon, Karen found herself rocking to the beat along with everyone else. She and Damian shared a smile, their heads bobbing in time with the music. By the time the concert ended, she felt more relaxed and in control.

"He's really good," she said as they filed out with the crowd. "I don't have any of his CDs, but I'm definitely adding him to my collection."

Damian nodded. "Marcus is very good. I have a couple of his CDs." Once they made it to an open area, he pulled her to the side. "It's still early, and I'm not ready for the evening to end. How about we go check out the club? Do you like to dance?"

"I do, but I haven't in a while." She checked her watch. It was only ten. "Sure. Let's do it." He reached for her hand and entwined their fingers as if it was the most natural thing to do. She felt the same heat as she had when they shook hands at lunch.

They heard the music as they rounded the corner. Damian immediately pulled her onto the dance floor. Karen swayed her hips in time with his, her eyes glued to every move he made—slim waist, washboard abs, muscular thighs and arms. She loved dancing, and it had been a long time since she allowed herself to be free and uninhibited. After a few up-tempo grooves, the music changed to a ballad. He moved closer and wrapped his arms around her waist, bringing her flush against his hard body.

She trembled when his hand came in contact with her bare back. Any calm she previously felt fled. His fingers moved slowly across the exposed area, searing a path on her skin. She glanced up to see his gaze locked on hers. Karen's breath caught, and her heart hammered in her chest. His eyes darkened, the green flecks more evident. His gaze drifted to her mouth, then back up to meet her eyes. She wanted him to kiss her. They'd only been together a few hours, yet the only thing on her mind was having his lips on hers. She turned away and rested her head on his shoulder, hoping he didn't see the longing in her eyes.

Damian couldn't stop the rampant desire flowing through his body. Sensations coursed through his veins, the likes of which he'd never experienced. Holding Karen in his arms and running his hands over the smooth expanse of her bare skin—it was softer than he anticipated—had him on the verge of doing something totally out of character, like tossing her over his shoulder and carting her off to the nearest bed. Her gloss-slicked lips appeared soft and inviting, and he wanted nothing more than to taste and nibble on them. Before she dropped her gaze, he read the same thing in her dark brown eyes.

The guilt he had felt earlier rose, but he pushed it down, reminding himself those feelings had no place here. He wasn't married anymore or in a relationship. He was free to explore this attraction between him and Karen. Damian closed his eyes, held her closer and inhaled the seductive scent of her perfume, letting the powerful sensations take over. He liked the way she fit in his arms, as if she belonged there. Though the thought scared him, he couldn't move away. He wanted to hold her this way all night.

As if by some unspoken communication, the DJ played three slow songs in a row. Damian offered up a silent thank-you and tightened his arms around her. Too soon, the music changed again. Karen lifted her head and stepped out of his embrace, and he instantly missed the closeness.

"Can I get you something to drink?" he asked.

"Yes, please."

He quickly claimed the table a couple had just vacated, and she sat. "What would you like?"

"A cosmo."

"Coming right up." He squeezed in at the black-and-white marble bar and gave their order. Several minutes later, he returned, drinks in hand. Damian placed her drink on the table in front of her and then sat in the chair across from her.

"What did you get?"

"Jack and Coke." His brow lifted when she took a long drink from the glass. "Good?"

She nodded and tilted the glass to her lips again before setting it on the table with a trembling hand.

He chuckled inwardly, thinking she might want to slow down. He picked up his own glass and took a small sip. "What brings you on the cruise? Vacation?"

"My best friend got married before the ship left on Saturday. Her new husband is performing, so they decided to make it part of their honeymoon."

"The woman you were with yesterday?" She nodded and he said, "I wish them many happy years together." A memory of his wedding day flashed in his head. "Who's the lucky guy?"

"Maybe you've heard of him. R & B singer and producer Monte."

"Really? I know of him. I once heard he planned to never marry."

"So did I. But Janae is the sweetest person I know, and I guess he couldn't resist."

"Is that why you were dressed up when I saw you?"

"Yes. What about you? Are you on vacation?"

"I guess you can say that." He laughed. "Actually, my two friends guilt-tripped me into coming. They bought the ticket and then asked if I was going to waste their money and accused me of not being a good friend." Karen laughed—a low, throaty sound that made his heart jump.

"That's wrong." She leaned forward with laughter shining in her eyes. "Were you being a bad friend?" she asked teasingly.

"Probably," he admitted. "I've turned down every offer to take a trip together for the last several years."

"Well, I'd say you redeemed yourself by coming on the cruise. You should be off the hook for at least a *month*."

Damian laughed. "Good point. I'll make sure to tell them that." They laughed together again, and then silence fell over the table. He hadn't laughed with a woman in a long time and enjoyed the easy rapport they seemed to be developing. He covered her hand with his. "I still wasn't too keen on coming, even after we boarded...until I saw you. I'm looking forward to whatever this week brings."

"So am I."

They finished their drinks, both lost in thought.

He gestured toward the dance area. "Are you ready to hit the dance floor again?"

"Let's do it."

He rose, assisted Karen from the chair and trailed her as she dipped in time with the beat out to the dance floor. She raised her arms in the air and danced with reckless abandon, her sensual movements sending bolts of white-hot desire shooting through him. Damian sucked in a sharp breath and tried to will his body calm. They danced to a few more songs. Then he suggested taking a walk.

Karen fanned herself. "Whew. I haven't danced like that in ages. And definitely not in these shoes."

He glanced down at the sexy jeweled sandals and her red-painted toenails. "But they look amazing."

"Thanks. Shoes are my weakness. I needed an extra bag just for them."

He shook his head and chuckled. Come to think of it, the shoes she had had on that first day were just as sexy. "You have good taste." They came to an exit. "Are you okay to walk on the deck for a little while? We won't stay long."

"Sure. I could use the fresh air."

He held the door open and let her precede him, then led her over to an empty spot at the rail. Neither spoke for several minutes. Damian studied her as she stared out into the black night—the shimmering glow of her skin bathed in the moonlight, the serene expression on her face. Their attraction had been instant and strong. Why her? And why now? He didn't think he would ever allow himself to get close to another woman, but in less than twenty-four hours, Karen had proven him wrong. She fascinated him. Called to him. Made him laugh and feel alive for the first time in years.

She looked up at him. "Penny for your thoughts."

"I was just thinking about you. Us. How much I'm enjoying your company."

She smiled. "You're not so bad yourself."

Damian reached up and stroked a finger down her cheek

and lowered his head. He hovered close enough for their breaths to mingle, waiting, seeking permission. She hesitated for a brief moment, then tilted her head upward. He touched his mouth to hers, once, twice. Her lips parted beneath his, and he slid his tongue inside. He hadn't kissed a woman like this in a while—five years to be exact—but it didn't take long for him to catch up. She tangled her tongue with his, and he groaned deep in his throat. He turned, leaned against the rail, widened his stance and pulled her between his legs.

Karen wrapped her arms around his neck, grabbed the back of his head and held him in place. Damian had no problem with that. He had no intention of letting go—not until he got his fill—which in his estimation might take all night. He angled his head and deepened the kiss. His hands roamed down her back, cupped her bottom and brought her flush against his erection. He wanted her to feel what she was doing to him. They stood there with their mouths fused for who knows how long until she shivered. He gave her one last kiss, then lifted his head.

"Cold?"

"A little," she said, shivering again.

He rubbed up and down her arms, leaned down and placed a soft kiss on her lips. "Let's get you inside."

She nodded.

Taking her hand, he led her back inside. "May I see you to your room?"

"I'd like that."

Her swollen, moist lips and passion-filled eyes tempted him beyond reason. "Lead the way." They walked to the elevator hand in hand. Luckily, no one else boarded, because he really needed to kiss her again, and he couldn't wait one more second. As soon as the doors closed, he backed her against the wall and slanted his mouth over hers. All too soon the distinctive chime sounded, signaling the elevator had reached her floor. Reluctantly, Damian ended the kiss.

He followed her down the hall until she stopped at a door, unlocked it and pushed it open.

She stepped inside and stared up at him. "Would you like to come in for a few minutes?"

Hell yeah, I want to come in. Leaning against the door frame, he said, "I'd better not. What are your plans for tomorrow? Are you going into Jamaica?"

She nodded. "I'm taking one of the tours to Dunn's River Falls, and it includes lunch afterward at a popular restaurant."

"Mind if we spend the day together? I really enjoy being with you."

"I don't mind at all. I booked the tour at eleven. Tomorrow night I'm going to Monte's show. He had seats reserved for us, but I can ask Janae to see if he can get another one, if you want to go."

"If you won't be tired of my company by then, I'd love to. How about we meet for breakfast in the morning?"

"Sure. I'll wait for you by the buffet entrance at eight-thirty."

"Sounds like a plan." Damian wanted to kiss her again but didn't trust himself to stay in control. He was having a hard enough time standing close to her without touching her. She took the decision out of his hands when she pulled him down for a kiss that stole his breath.

"Thanks for a wonderful evening, Damian. I'll see you in the morning."

He kissed her softly. "Good night, Karen. Sweet dreams."

She backed into the room and closed the door softly. He stood with his hand on the door.

Damian wanted to make love to her.

The realization shook him to his core. Not so much that

he had the urge, but how strongly he felt it. He had been celibate for five years by choice because he hadn't found a woman who excited him. Karen more than excited him. She intrigued him like no other woman before. Including his late wife.

He hadn't accepted her invitation tonight, but if she offered tomorrow, he wouldn't turn her down. And he would be prepared.

Chapter 4

Damian went back to the deck, gripped the railing and gulped in a lungful of crisp ocean air. The startling depth of his desire for Karen had thrown him for a loop. How could he want a woman so much? And in such a short time. He could still smell her intoxicating perfume, feel her silky skin beneath his fingers and taste the sweetness of her kiss in his mouth. As much as he wanted to take Karen up on her offer, he needed to step back and gain some perspective. His mind said things were moving too fast, but his body argued they weren't moving fast enough. Even now his heart hadn't returned to a normal pace, and his erection throbbed with desire. Damian was tempted to go back and knock on her door. He hadn't accepted her invitation tonight, one, because he felt it was too soon, and two, he didn't have any protection. Troy and Kyle mentioned they had left him some condoms, and he made a mental note to check his bag when he returned to his room.

He remembered he needed to sign up for the tour in Jamaica and glanced down at his watch. Leaving the deck, he retraced his steps and searched out the tour desk, hoping it hadn't closed. Luckily it hadn't, and there were three spaces available for the eleven o'clock tour. He was too wound up to sleep and made his way to the piano bar, where an up-and-coming artist was playing. Damian claimed a stool at the circular bar, signaled the bartender and ordered a Coke.

"Thanks," he said, accepting the glass. Although his body had calmed considerably, his mind continued to race with thoughts of Karen.

"Excuse me. Is this seat taken?"

His head came up. A woman stood next to him wearing a white low-cut skintight bodysuit and offering a come-hither smile.

"Be my guest." He gestured to the stool, then went back to his drink.

She slid onto the stool, purposely leaning close enough to brush her breasts against his arm.

Damian pretended not to notice. He didn't want to give the woman any indication he might be interested. She tried making small talk, and he remained courteous, but after a few minutes began to think he should have gone to his room.

"So, does that empty left hand mean you're not married?"

He stared down at his hand. He'd finally stopped wearing his ring a year ago, and the tan line had faded completely, as if nothing had ever been there. "No, I'm not."

She scooted closer. "Are you looking to be?"

"No."

"Are you sure? A handsome guy like you looks like he should be married." Her hand skimmed his thigh, sliding upward. He clamped his hand down on hers and jumped from the stool. "I think I'm going to call it a night."

Her gaze raked over him. "Want some company?"

"No, thanks. Enjoy the cruise." He turned on his heel and strode out of the lounge. Damian scrubbed a hand down his face. While he didn't mind an assertive woman, overaggressiveness turned him off. He hadn't gone far when a hand touched his shoulder.

He groaned inwardly, thinking the woman had followed

him. Glancing over his shoulder, he was relieved to see his friends.

"Well, well. For somebody who didn't want to come on this cruise, you sure have been busy," Kyle said.

"What's up?"

Troy folded his arms across his chest. "That's what we want to know about you. We haven't seen you all day."

Kyle laughed. "My man D has jumped back into the game at full speed. I saw the woman in the catsuit. Hot! Curves for days. She basically handed herself to you on a platter."

"I wasn't interested."

"Is that because you're more interested in the woman you were dancing with earlier?" Troy asked.

"Damn, were you guys following me around or something?"

Troy shook his head. "No. We went looking for some fun and just happened to see you while we were dancing. She's the same woman you were staring at the first day?"

He nodded. "We're spending the day together in Jamaica tomorrow, then going to Monte's performance tomorrow night."

"I guess you didn't need our help after all," Kyle said with a laugh. He lowered his voice. "Those condoms are in the small inner pocket of your duffel bag...in case you were wondering."

Yeah, he *had* wondered. "Are you guys going into Jamaica?"

"Yeah," Kyle answered. "You think you can tear yourself away from your new friend long enough to hang with your *old* friends once we get to the Bahamas?"

He really wanted to spend as much time with Karen as possible since they had limited time together. However, even though they worked together, he had neglected his friendship with Kyle and Troy, and they did pay for the cruise. "Yeah, man."

They said their goodbyes, and Damian continued to his room. Once there, he showered and crawled into bed. An hour later, he lay awake with thoughts of Karen filling his head. Where was she from? What did she do? Did she feel the chemistry between them as strongly as he did? He planned to get the answers to those questions and more. Turning over, he made himself comfortable and closed his eyes. Morning couldn't come soon enough.

Karen untangled herself from the sheets and groaned. Another dream. Her pulse raced, and her breathing came in short gasps. It was the second one she'd had tonight, and seemed so real she would swear Damian lay beside her with his lips pressed against the hollow of her neck. She hadn't been able to get his kisses out of her mind, or the feel of his hands sliding over her bare back and hips.

Scooting off the bed, she went into the bathroom and splashed some water on her face in an effort to cool off. She walked back into the room, opened the curtain slightly and leaned against the door frame. The sun had already begun its ascent, breaking through the early gray morning with streaks of red, orange and pink. Her mind lingered over every detail since she had met Damian, from their flirting at the pool and the uncertainty in his voice when he asked her out, to his solicitous manner during the concert and the possessive way he'd held her while his mouth plundered hers.

She wanted him. Bad. So much that she had invited him into her room last night, something she would never do with a man she'd just met. Maybe the effects of the alcohol she'd consumed had lowered her inhibitions. No. It was the man, plain and simple. But he hadn't accepted her invitation, and Karen wondered why, when he clearly seemed to be as into her as she was into him, not to mention the huge erection she'd felt pressed against her belly.

Maybe she had read more into what was happening between them, or maybe he thought her too aggressive. She sighed softly. Whatever the case, she needed to apologize. She didn't want Damian to think she made a habit of inviting strange men into her room.

Pushing away from the sliding glass door, Karen went to get ready for breakfast. She dug out her black swimsuit. The sexy cutout one-piece had crisscrossing straps across the back, but aside from that, left her back and sides bare, and tied at the hips. She put it on and slipped into a black crochet cover-up. Grabbing her tote, she added her waterproof camera, a change of clothes, towel, comb, brush and wallet, then sat on a chair to fasten the straps on her flat sandals. She picked up the tote and room key and left.

Karen searched the dining room for Damian and spotted him waving. She started in his direction, then halted her steps when he came toward her wearing a black tank exposing his strong muscular shoulders and arms, black swim trunks and sandals. An involuntary moan slipped from her lips. The man exuded masculinity in waves. It would be harder than she thought to keep her desire under control. As she came closer, his gaze traveled over her, stopped at her breasts and then slid lower, just below her stomach. His eyes darkened with desire, sending a rush of heat directly to her core.

"Morning," Damian said, dipping his head to kiss her cheek.

His soft, warm lips lingered on her cheek, and a shiver passed through her. "Good morning. Have you been waiting long?"

"No. Just a few minutes." He led her to the table. "Why don't you leave your bag here and go fix your plate? I'll get mine when you come back."

"Okay." Karen surveyed the buffet and filled her plate with a small amount of scrambled eggs, potatoes with onions and peppers, two strips of crisp bacon and a slice of toast, then got a glass of orange juice. She placed her plate on the table, and Damian shook his head. "What?"

"That's all you're eating?"

She glanced down at the plate. "Yes, why?"

"I can still see half of your plate."

"I may go back for more."

He nodded, leaned down close to her ear and whispered huskily, "By the way, you're killing me with that outfit. Makes me want to cancel the tour." His mouth curved in a wicked grin, he winked and walked off.

The timbre of his voice and accompanying look turned her legs to jelly. Karen managed to pull out her chair and drop down in it before she collapsed. She fanned herself and took a long sip of juice.

Damian returned to the table with his plate piled high—French toast, scrambled eggs, potatoes, bacon, sausage and fruit.

"You can go back for more, you know. That's why they call it a buffet."

He paused with the saltshaker in his hand. "What? I don't have that much."

"Whatever you say," she said with a laugh, and forked up a portion of potatoes.

He wiggled his eyebrows. "I have a healthy appetite. What can I say?"

Her belly fluttered with the double meaning. She propped her chin in her hand and leaned forward. "So do I."

"That's good to know," he murmured.

Damian tried to concentrate on his breakfast. Their verbal exchange, combined with the revealing black cover she wore over her bathing suit, had him hard as a steel beam and he was tempted, once again, to drag her to the nearest bed and find out just how healthy of an appetite she had. He had never engaged in this type of sensual play with his late wife—she had been very reserved when it came to sex. But he knew things would be different with Karen. He sensed a passion and fire in her that he eagerly wanted to explore. He forced his thoughts elsewhere and finished breakfast.

"Are you ready to head out?" he asked when her plate was empty.

"Yes."

He stood, slung his backpack over his shoulder and helped Karen. More than one man turned when she walked by. Damian moved closer and placed a possessive hand on the small of her back. Sending a lethal glare at one man who was staring a little too long, he guided her toward the ship's exit.

The ship's coordinator checked off their names, gave them colored wristbands and directed them to a waiting van.

"Damian," Karen started, once they were en route, "I want to apologize about last night."

"For what?"

"The whole room invitation thing. I've never done anything like that before," she mumbled, and turned to stare out the window.

He turned her face back toward his. "You don't have to apologize. If it helps any, I really wanted to accept your invitation, but I didn't want to come on too strong."

He placed his arm around her shoulders, kissed her forehead and pulled her closer. They rode the rest of the way in silence. After reaching the park and getting water shoes, he suggested they rent a locker. Damian stripped off his shirt, placed it in his bag and put it in the locker.

"If you—" His eyes widened, and his mouth fell open.

Karen had taken off the cover and stood clad in a bathing suit that left every inch of her velvety brown back and sides bare. The sight almost dropped him to his knees. A man passing by whispered, *"Dayuum!"* while staring with his jaw unhinged. Damian couldn't blame the man, because she was a vision of beauty. He let his gaze roam lazily over every delectable curve.

She placed her tote in the locker and faced him. "Were you going to say something?"

He stared at her with confusion, then realized she had asked him a question. He shook his head. "I'm sorry. What did you ask?"

"I thought you were going to say something."

For the life of him, he couldn't remember one word. "Nothing. You look *amazing*."

She slowly looked him up and down. "So do you."

It's going to be a long day. He closed the locker and reached for her hand. "We'd better get going."

At the base of the fall, a vendor asked if they wanted their picture taken.

"Yes. Take two." He wanted a memory of this trip with her. The photographer took the pictures of them together, then one of them separately.

"You can view the pictures on your way out and buy if you like," the man said.

Once they started the climb, Damian took a picture of Karen using the waterproof camera she'd brought along. Instead of linking hands and climbing with the others, they chose to leisurely climb to the top, stopping to linger in some of the pools along the way. Unable to resist, Damian came up behind Karen, wrapped his arm around her and trailed kisses along the smooth flesh of her neck and shoulders. She moaned softly. Turning her in his arms, he transferred his kisses to her jaw and nibbled on her lush bottom lip until her lips parted. He kissed her hungrily. Her hands came up and circled his neck.

"I can't get enough of kissing you," he managed to say huskily against her lips before kissing her again.

"Damian," she whispered, her body trembling.

He pressed his lips to her temple, squeezed his eyes shut and tried to slow his galloping heart. Damian had never been so tempted by a woman in his life and certainly hadn't ever lost control this way. He opened his eyes, eased back and released her. Giving her one last kiss, he took her hand and gestured her forward. "Come on, baby. Let's keep going."

Karen didn't know how he expected her to climb anything after kissing her senseless. Her legs felt like rubber, her heart raced and her mind was a jumbled mess. She took a moment to collect herself before climbing the next step. They moved at a good pace for a while, and she stopped along the way to take a few pictures to show her students. After taking the last shot, she turned and lost her footing.

Damian tightened his grip on her waist. "Careful, sweetheart."

The low timbre of his voice in her ear and the heat of his touch wreaked havoc on her nerves. She sucked in a shaky breath. "I'm good." She glanced up. "We're almost at the top."

Once they reached the top, she turned and looked down with her arms spread. "That was great. I can't wait to get back and see the pictures."

He nodded. "I'm glad you allowed me to tag along. How about we get changed, stop and pick up the pictures, then get back to the van? It'll be leaving shortly for lunch."

"Okay." They retrieved their belongings from the locker and headed to the changing facilities.

"I'll wait for you over by the lockers," Damian said.

She nodded and watched his sexy stroll until he disappeared. "Mmm, mmm, mmm."

Inside, Karen stripped off her soaked bathing suit, dried off and dressed in shorts and a tank top. She combed out her wet hair and secured it back into a ponytail. She met Damian, and they returned the water shoes, paid for the pictures and boarded the van taking them to the restaurant.

"You didn't have to pay for the pictures, Damian," she said once the van pulled off.

"Think of it as my way of saying thank you. I can't remember the last time I enjoyed myself so much. I'll never forget it," he said, holding her eyes with an intensity that made her insides tremble.

"Neither will I." She stared down at the picture of them in her hands. At least she would have something to remember him by when the cruise ended. But for some reason, the thought of never seeing him again caused a churning in her stomach.

Chapter 5

Karen and Damian entered the open-air restaurant known for its jerk chicken and placed their order. They laughed and talked about everything from the Jamaican sights and weather to music and politics—everything except themselves—while waiting for their food. It took a while for it to arrive, but it was well worth the wait. She bit into the spicy, crispy chicken, and an involuntary moan slipped from her lips.

Damian lifted an eyebrow and chuckled. "Good?"

"Oh, yes. Don't take my word for it. Try it yourself."

He picked up a piece of chicken from his plate and tried it. Nodding, he finished chewing. "Mmm, it is good."

They ate in silence for several minutes. She scooped up some of the rice and peas, loving the subtle peppery flavor.

"Did you enjoy climbing the falls?" he asked between bites.

"Loved it."

"Are you always this adventurous?"

She shrugged. "I'll try anything once. Well, except bungee jumping. *That* will not be happening."

He threw his head back and roared with laughter.

"What? All I can think about is that cord snapping, along with my neck."

Still chuckling, Damian picked up his drink and took a sip. "That's not on my list, either, though I never quite thought about it like that."

"What about you? Do you like adventure?"

"I used to," he answered softly. His voice held a hint of sadness.

"Any reason why you don't anymore?"

He smiled faintly. "Working too hard, I guess."

"Well, I'm glad you decided to join me," she said, trying to lift his mood. "Sounds like you need to get out more."

Holding her gaze, he said, "Maybe. I haven't had this much fun in ages." He covered her hand. "I'm looking forward to much more."

"So am I."

They continued eating, and then he asked, "So, Karen, what do you do?"

She paused with the fork in her hand. The last man she had dated didn't think teaching met the standards of a successful career. What would Damian think? Karen halted her thoughts. She didn't care what anyone thought—she loved teaching. "I teach."

"Really?"

She stilled. "Is there something wrong with teaching?"

"Not at all. I think teachers are hardworking, dedicated and severely underpaid."

Relaxing, she laughed. "Me, too."

"What grade do you teach?"

"Fourth."

He shook his head. "You must have the patience of a saint."

"Some days it's a struggle, but I love it."

"I'm sure you're a phenomenal educator."

"Thanks. What about you?"

"I work for a consulting firm."

Before she could question him further, the driver indicated it was time to leave. They discarded the remnants of their lunch, followed their group out and rode the short distance back to the ship. As they boarded and made their way to the elevators, Karen tried to cover a yawn.

"Tired?"

"A little." She checked her watch—two-thirty. "Oh, by the way, you're good to go on the concert tonight if you still want to."

"You still offering?" Damian pushed the elevator button.

"I am. The show starts at eight." She got in the elevator, and he followed.

"Thanks. What're you going to do until then?"

"Shower, wash my hair and probably take a nap. Are you going to meet your friends?"

"I'll probably relax for a little while, then see if I can find them."

The elevator opened, and he followed her to her room. She unlocked the door and then turned back.

"I'll pick you up at seven-thirty. Is that all right?"

"That's fine."

"See you in a little while." He bent low and placed a gentle kiss on her lips. "Sleep well." Then he was gone.

After showering and taking a short nap, Damian went in search of Troy and Kyle and found them in the casino playing blackjack.

Troy looked up from his cards. "What's up? I see you got our message. I was wondering if you'd show up."

"How long you guys been playing?"

"Long enough to lose damn near all my money," Kyle grumbled, turning over his cards and showing another busted hand.

Damian laughed. "I'm glad I got here when I did. I need to keep my money."

"Please, you have almost as much money as Midas."

"Yeah, right. And you don't? Kyle, you have more money than Troy and I put together."

"That's because Kyle is a miser," Troy said and signaled the dealer to give him another card.

"It's called managing your money properly," Kyle said, mimicking the nasally tone of their high school economics teacher.

They looked at each other and broke out in laughter. Back in high school, they had teased Mr. Cornwell and laughed behind his back, but the three friends had taken the man's words to heart, made some lucrative investments and were now financially well-off. Doing this had also given them the freedom to start their own business when they were ready for career changes.

"How was Dunn's River Falls?" Kyle asked.

Damian smiled, remembering how good Karen looked in her swimsuit, how smooth her skin felt and how much he liked kissing her. "Great."

"That good?"

Damian nodded.

Troy lifted an eyebrow. "You're not planning to back out on us tomorrow, are you?"

"Nah, man. But I am going with her to Monte's show tonight. Front row, reserved seats. Remember when we saw her dressed up that first day?"

"Yeah," they both answered.

"Karen's best friend had just gotten married to Monte. So he reserved some seats."

Kyle threw down another busted hand. "I think I've lost enough money for one day." He stood. "Let's go listen to some music and grab something to eat, and then Damian can tell us all about *Karen*."

They filed out of the casino and caught a performance in the atrium. There was no room on the main floor, so they ended up going to the next level. Afterward, over an early dinner, they lamented the fact that so many great singing artists, like the one they'd just heard, were going the independent route. With radio stations and music companies looking for quick money, the market seemed to be flooded with cookie-cutter mediocre talent.

The conversation turned to Karen. "I don't know much about her, except that she's a teacher," Damian said.

"Did you tell her you used to teach?" Troy asked before forking up a piece of steak.

"No. I just told her I work for a consulting firm."

"Good move," Kyle said, toasting Damian with his wineglass. "You don't need to divulge all your secrets to somebody you probably won't see again."

"Hmm." For some reason, the knowledge that he might not see Karen again after this week bothered him, but he decided not to share that piece of information with his friends. He wanted to learn more about her. One week wouldn't be nearly enough time for him to uncover all he needed to know. But it was a start. He checked his watch and realized he had less than an hour to change before meeting Karen. He finished his meal and stood. "What time do you want to meet in the morning?"

Troy shrugged. "Say breakfast at eight, and we leave around nine?"

"Okay. What are we doing?"

Kyle and Troy shared a smile. Kyle said, "You just need to bring a couple of changes of clothes. We plan to have a good time."

Damian divided a wary gaze between the two men. "What are you two up to?"

"Just want you to enjoy yourself," Troy answered. He chuckled. "We may never get you out of the house again, so we have to pack it in while we can."

Though Troy had said the comment in a teasing manner, Damian couldn't stop the guilt that arose. They had been friends since middle school, and Damian could always count on the two of them to have his back no matter what. "I'll be ready."

In his room, Damian changed into tailored slacks, a silk polo and loafers. Thinking he might not get back until late, he filled his oversize backpack with the clothes he'd need for tomorrow's excursion and placed it on a chair. He pulled the duffel bag from the closet and searched for the condoms. He found them, tore off a few and put them in his wallet. Taking a quick look at his watch, he picked up the card key, slipped it into his pocket and left to pick up Karen.

When she opened the door, he could only stare.

"Hey, come on in. Let me grab my purse." She walked a few steps, slipped her arms into a sheer cover-up, turned back and chuckled. "Damian, are you coming in?"

Shaking himself, he followed her. "Sorry. Every time I see you, you take my breath away." She wore another sexy dress paired with matching sandals.

She smiled. "Thanks. You look pretty good yourself." She slung a purse over her shoulder. "I'm ready."

So was he.

In the elevator, Karen closed her eyes briefly and drew in a deep breath. The heat in Damian's eyes threatened to incinerate her. The chemistry between them increased exponentially each time they were together, and she didn't know how much longer they'd last before the intense desire overtook them. She glanced up to find his eyes fixed on hers. His gaze drifted to her mouth, and she subconsciously licked her lips, remembering the warm slide of his tongue against hers. Just as he reached for her, the ding of the elevator sounded.

Damian leaned close to her ear and murmured, "To be continued." He wrapped a hand around her waist and steered her around the crowd waiting to board, down the hall toward the theater.

Karen tried to put some space between them, but he held firm to her, the warmth of his strong fingers penetrating the silky material of her top. Just like earlier, his touch did things to her insides and made her have visions of the two of them naked and writhing in a bed. She pushed the dangerous thoughts from her head and kept walking. They met Janae coming from another direction.

The two women embraced. "Hey, Karen," Janae said. "Nice to see you again, Damian."

"Same here. Congratulations on your marriage."

"Thanks. How was Jamaica?"

Karen smiled. "Good."

"Very good," Damian reiterated.

Janae divided a speculative glance between Karen and Damian, then threw a look at Karen that said she wanted details.

Ignoring the look, Karen said, "Dunn's River Falls was great. You and Terrence will have to go when you come back."

"Is that so?" she asked with a smile. "Maybe we will."

They joined the line of people entering the theater. "Do you know where we're sitting?"

"Donovan said he'd be waiting near the front." As soon as they were seated, Janae leaned over and whispered, "What's going on with you and Damian?"

She looked over to where Damian stood talking to Donovan, and then back to Janae. "We're enjoying each other's company, that's all."

"Hmph. Girl, the way he looked at you when I asked about Jamaica said he was enjoying more than that. I think he likes you."

"I like him, too. He seems nice."

"Nooo, I mean he *really* likes you."

Karen waved a dismissive hand. "Please, we just met."

Janae shook her head. "Okay, Miss In Denial. Mark my words, the man is interested in far more than just hanging out with you for this week."

"He's just… I don't know."

"Sounds a lot like the way I was feeling about Terrence when we first met." She laughed. "You do remember what happened the first time we went to Terrence's concert, don't you?"

She stared, confused.

"One of us ended up married."

"What does that have to do with me and Damian? You and Terrence are in love."

"We didn't start off that way. Remember when we used to talk about how sensual *Monte's* music and lyrics were?"

"Yeah?"

"All I'm going to say is this new music is even more so. And the fireworks between you and Damian are enough to supply an entire Fourth of July celebration. Mark my words, there are going to be a lot of couples behind closed doors tonight, including y'all." She gave Karen a knowing look when Damian took his seat, and then leaned back with a smug smile.

Karen didn't comment. She knew exactly what Janae meant. In the past, music had been part of the foreplay when she and Andre made love. Her attraction to Damian far exceeded that of her ex, and it wouldn't take much for her to lose control—music or not. She hazarded a glimpse his way and found him seemingly deep in thought. He frowned briefly, and a shadow flickered across his face. *I wonder what that was about.* His voice broke into her thoughts.

"You're frowning. Is something wrong?"

"No," she said hastily. "Just thinking. It's nothing."

He studied her a moment. "You sure?"

"Yes." She reached down and gave his hand a reassuring squeeze.

He lifted it and placed a lingering kiss on the back. Smiling, he laced their fingers together and trained his eyes on the stage.

Karen turned and met Janae's smiling face.

Janae mouthed, *I told you.*

Soon the lights dimmed, and Monte hit the stage and greeted the audience. "Before we get started, I'd like my beautiful wife to join me."

Gasps and expressions of shock flooded the room. "Did you know he was going to do this, Janae?" Karen asked.

She nodded. "Yes. He promised it would be the only time." Janae stood, and Donovan escorted her to the stage.

While holding Janae's hand, Monte sang a beautiful ballad he had composed just for her, expressing the depths of his love. He looked at her with such emotion that it brought tears to Karen's eyes. She wondered how it would feel to have a man look at her that way.

A tear slid down her cheek. Damian gently wiped it away with the pad of his thumb before she could react. The tender and sweet gesture caught her by surprise, and the tears came faster.

Damian draped his arm around her shoulders and pressed a kissed to her temple. "Are you all right?"

"Yes," she said, sniffing. "I'm just happy for Janae, and the words to the song are so beautiful."

"He must love her a lot."

"He does, and she loves him just as much."

He stared at her for a lengthy minute with a strange look on his face before turning his attention back to the stage.

She wiped away the lingering tears, grateful that she hadn't worn mascara or eyeliner. She and Janae shared a smile when Janae returned; then Karen tuned in for the rest of the show. Monte sang a mixture of the old and new, and she found Janae's description of the new music quite accurate. He could have titled it *The Ultimate Make-Out CD*. By the show's end, she noticed more than a few couples snuggling closer.

Karen and Damian said their goodbyes to Janae, and he convinced her to take another walk. Outside, they strolled hand in hand along the deck, neither speaking. She marveled at how comfortable she felt with him. In the short time since she'd met him, he'd impressed her as a gentleman. He had a great sense of humor and a way about him she couldn't put into words that drew her as no other man had before. Why couldn't they have met under different circumstances? He stopped walking abruptly.

"Karen, I…" He wrapped his arm around her and pulled her into his embrace at the same time his head descended.

He kissed her with a potency that weakened her knees. She slid her arms around his neck and held him in place as his hands moved slowly up and down her back, caressing and teasing. His lips left her mouth and skated along her jaw before claiming her mouth again. At length, he lifted his head but didn't release her. She read the question in his eyes, knew what he was asking. She came up on her toes and kissed him.

Reaching for his hand, Karen led him back to her room. When they reached it, she slid the key in, unlocked the door and glanced back at Damian. Once they crossed the threshold, she knew there would be no turning back.

Chapter 6

Damian shut the door behind him and took a cursory glance around the suite. He noted an end table, a sofa and a small bistro-like table with two chairs on one side of the room. But what held his attention was the king-size bed on the opposite side of the room. Karen removed the top she had worn over the dress, then tossed it and her purse on the sofa. She wrung her hands together and looked everywhere except at him.

He placed his hands on her shoulders and turned her to face him. "Second thoughts?"

She shook her head hastily. "No."

"Are you sure? Karen, we don't have—"

She placed her finger on his lips. "I'm sure."

He captured her hand, kissed the center of her palm and wrist, then trailed kisses along her arm up to her shoulder. Moving closer, Damian tilted her chin, flicked his tongue against the corners of her mouth and nibbled on the lush fullness of her bottom lip.

"Damian," Karen said on a breathless sigh.

Hearing his name whispered from her lips spiked his arousal. Her mouth parted slightly, and his tongue found hers. He plunged deep, swirling and feasting on the sweetness like a starved man. His hands moved down her back, over her hips and around to gently knead her firm breasts. She trembled beneath his touch, fueling his passion, and the kiss intensified. Her hands came up to stroke the nape of his neck, and he groaned deep in his throat.

Karen tore her mouth away, breathing harshly.

Running his fingers lightly over the exposed area above her breasts, he asked, "Do you know how beautiful you are?" He bent and replaced his fingers with his tongue, the scent of her seductive perfume filling his nostrils and arousing him further. He had fantasized about being here with her like this almost from the moment they met. Damian swept her in his arms, covered the short distance to the bed in three strides and deposited her in the center. He kicked off his shoes and climbed onto the bed.

"You wear the sexiest shoes," he murmured. He lifted her leg, placed a lingering kiss on her ankle, undid the strap and slid the shoe off. He lifted her other leg and repeated the gesture.

She moaned softly, and the sound almost snapped his control. He closed his eyes to steady his breathing and maintain control. It had been five long years since he'd been intimate with a woman, and he was close to exploding.

Starting at her feet, he caressed and kissed his way up her body. He pulled her into a sitting position, reached behind her neck and released the clasp on her dress. The material fell away, pooling at her waist. Karen leaned back on her elbows and lifted her hips so Damian could slide the dress down and off, leaving her clad in a very sexy strapless purple lace bra and matching bikini panties. His breath stalled in his lungs. "Exquisite," he murmured while skimming his fingers over her hip. He left the bed, draped the dress over a chair and feasted his eyes on her loveliness. He pulled his shirt hem from his pants.

Karen scooted to the edge of the bed and stood. "Allow me."

He stood still while she eased the shirt up and over his head, then laid it on top of her dress. Her hands moved over his chest and stomach, electrifying him in the process. His breaths came in short gasps, and his muscles contracted beneath her touch. She moved her hand lower and stroked him through his slacks. His knees almost buckled, and he released a guttural moan. Damian endured the sweet torture a moment longer, then took a step back and undid his belt.

Karen followed his move, pressed a kiss to his chest and said, "I got this, baby." She unbuttoned his pants and lowered the zipper, and they dropped to the floor. She kneeled down for him to step out and added them to the pile of clothes. Standing, she eyed him seductively and smiled. "Very impressive."

He chuckled softly, wrapped his arms around her and nipped at her ear. "You think so?"

"Absolutely. With this body, you could grace every month in a hunk calendar. Did you play sports?"

He eased back and twirled her slowly. "I don't know about that, but you…" He shook his head. "Definitely. And yes, I played basketball in high school and college." He kissed her. "No more talking. Right now I need you naked and in my arms."

"Then what are you waiting for?"

In the blink of an eye, he had her naked and on the bed. Damian removed his underwear, crawled onto the bed and lowered himself onto her. He shuddered from the pleasure of feeling their bodies skin-to-skin. He kissed her with a hunger that both excited and frightened him, and she returned his kiss, giving as good as she got. He kissed his way down to her beautifully formed breasts and captured a chocolate-tipped nipple between his lips. He laved and suckled first one, then the other. He charted a path down the front of her body with his hand and slid two fingers into her slick, wet heat until she was writhing and moaning beneath him.

Karen leaned up and skated her tongue over his jaw, neck and shoulder. Her hands ignited an inferno in his body as they traveled down his back.

Damian was nearing the end of his control. He withdrew his fingers, slid off the bed and searched for his wallet. He took the condoms out, tore one off and tossed the other ones onto the nightstand. After rolling it on, he moved over her, grinding his body against her. They both moaned. "It's been a while, so I'm apologizing up front if things go a little fast the first time. But I promise to make it up to you."

"I'm holding you to that."

He shifted his body and eased into her warmth until he was buried to the hilt. He held himself still, savoring the feeling of her tight walls surrounding him. "You feel so good, baby," he whispered against her lips at the same time he started moving inside her.

"Mmm. So do you."

He closed his eyes and let the sensations take over as he kept up the relaxed pace.

Karen wrapped her legs around his waist and pulled his mouth down on hers, their tongues tangling and dancing.

Damian lifted her hips as he plunged deeper and faster. Her whimpers and cries of passion excited him in a way he had never experienced and couldn't explain. He gritted his teeth, feeling her nails biting into the skin on his back, but didn't slow.

"Damian!" She arched off the bed and screamed his name. Her body shook, and her inner muscles contracted, clamping around him like a vise.

He threw back his head and exploded in a rush of pleasure that tore through him like a crack of lightning. His eyes slid closed, he groaned her name and shuddered above her as the spasms racked his body. She reached up and stroked the sides of his face. He opened his eyes, and when their eyes connected, he felt it—a little tug on his heart. This was more than just sex. Damian dismissed the thought, leaned down and kissed her tenderly. He rolled to his side, taking her with him, and held her snugly against his body. After several minutes, their ragged breathing returned to normal.

Karen basked in the contentment she felt in Damian's arms. Her body still hummed with desire. Even now, as his hand idly stroked her hip, she could feel her passions rising again. Then his caresses became more purposeful, and her breathing increased. He lifted her leg over his and trailed his hand along her inner thigh and up to her core, where she was already wet. She moaned when his fingers slipped inside and began stroking her. He probed deeper, and she moved her hips in time with his rhythm. "Yes, yes, *yes*," she chanted. His fingers moved faster and faster. Her breaths came in short gasps, and her legs trembled. She arched her head back, closed her eyes and bucked against his hand, crying out wildly as an orgasm ripped through her. Before she could recover, he rotated his fingers and did *something*. Her eyes flew open, her body went rigid and she came again, seized by a rush of sensation so intense she thought she might pass out. As she lay gasping for air, Damian lowered his head and kissed her. She moaned against his mouth and circled her arm around his neck.

He withdrew his fingers, rolled over and grabbed another condom. He tore open the package, and she took it from him. Sitting up, Karen straddled his thighs and rolled the condom slowly over his engorged shaft.

He sucked in a sharp breath. "Sweetheart, what are you doing to me?"

She smiled seductively. "Getting ready to go for a little ride. You mind?"

His eyes lit with desire. "Not at all. Ride on."

She held his gaze as she lowered herself inch by exquisite inch until he was embedded deeply within her. She shuddered, reveling in the way he filled her completely. Karen ran her hands over the strong, muscular planes of his chest and abdomen. The sun had darkened his golden skin to a warm bronze. Leaning down, she flicked her tongue against his lips. With lightning speed, Damian grasped the back of her head and crushed his mouth to hers, kissing her with an eroticism that made her head spin.

"Mmm. You're something else," he said.

She braced her hands on his shoulders and whispered against his lips, "You might want to hold on."

He chuckled low and sexy. "Show me what you've got, baby."

Karen lifted off him until only the tip of his shaft remained. Holding his gaze, she slowly lowered back down and rotated her hips in a figure-eight movement. She repeated the motion several times. The look of pure ecstasy on Damian's face was like nothing she had ever seen and turned her on even more. He kneaded her breasts, pushed them together and leaned up to take the sensitive peaks of her nipples in his mouth, sending jolts of pleasure to her core.

"No more teasing," he growled, gripping her hips, lifting the lower part of his body off the bed and thrusting deep.

She caught his driving rhythm and rode him hard. He pounded into her, and their cries of passion filled the room. Soon desire unlike anything she had ever known consumed her, and she flung her head back and screamed his name.

He tightened his grip on her hips and thrust faster. Damian tensed, and then his body bucked beneath hers as he shouted her name.

Karen collapsed over his chest and felt the rapid pace

of his heart matching hers. "I don't think I can move," she moaned.

His hands glided over her sweat-slicked skin. "Fine by me. I happen to like where you are right now."

So did she…a little too much. Gradually their breathing slowed and she drifted off.

Damian awakened hours later and stared down at the woman cuddled next to him with the sheets twisted around their lower bodies. His gaze lingered over her exposed naked body bathed in the morning sunlight peeking through the partially open curtains. He couldn't get enough of her. After that second round, their first attempt to shower had ended with her hands braced against the wall as he entered her from behind. Then they wound up in one of the chairs before showering again and falling asleep.

Something was happening between them—something more than sex. He had felt it when they made love and during their conversations. Troy had been right. Damian couldn't remember the last time he had smiled and laughed so much. He and Karen had a lot of things in common—everything from music to sports to food. Though they talked, they hadn't let their guards down enough to discuss more personal topics. Other than what she revealed to him over lunch, he still didn't know much about her. Had she been married before? What did she like to do outside the classroom?

Over the past two days, the parts of him that had lain dormant for so many years surfaced and burst free. When he was younger, he had hiked, sailed, danced, laughed and enjoyed life. Karen was the first woman who seemed to possess the same zeal for life as him. The other women he dated wouldn't have been caught dead doing any activity that required more than lifting a wineglass to their lips. The other thing that crossed his mind was her calming presence. For as long as he could remember, he'd be lucky if he slept for more than two hours at a time. Last night he had slept five hours straight without any of the restlessness that usually plagued him.

Damian glanced over his shoulder at the clock. He still had a couple of hours before meeting his friends. He eased out of her embrace, slid off the bed and headed for the bathroom. She stirred for a moment and then turned over and settled down. While in the bathroom, he found a new toothbrush and toothpaste in a gift basket on the counter. After finishing, he returned to find Karen awake and propped on her elbow. She had pulled the sheet up, covering her amazing body.

"Good morning," he said with a smile. "Did you sleep well?"

"Good morning. I did. How about you?"

"It was the best sleep I've had in a long time."

She stared at him curiously, then asked, "Are you done in the bathroom?"

He nodded. His eyes were riveted to her lush curves as she passed him, and his body reacted in kind. He was sitting up in bed with the sheet draped across his lower body when she returned.

Flipping the cover back, he patted the space next to him. "Come join me." She scooted next to him, and he wrapped his arms around her. Damian tilted her chin and kissed her. "Now, that's a good-morning kiss."

"Mmm, I agree."

"Are you going to be busy tonight with your friends?"

"We didn't really make any concrete plans. Why?"

"I want to have dinner with you," he said while nibbling on the shell of her ear. "We only have a couple of days left on the cruise, and I want to spend as much time with you as I can."

"In that case, okay."

"Seven good for you?"

"Absolutely."

Damian lowered his head and kissed her again. He had only meant it to be gentle—a kiss sealing the date—but the moment he touched her lips, he was lost. He tumbled her backward on the bed and deepened the kiss while his hands roamed possessively over her body.

"Don't you need to meet your friends?" Karen murmured against his lips.

"Mmm-hmm. I have plenty of time for them. Right now I just want to concentrate on you and this beautiful body of yours."

He reached for the last condom on the nightstand, quickly sheathed himself and slid into her sweet warmth. He wanted to take his time, but the way her muscles tightened around him and the sound of her calling his name in that sexy voice were his undoing. Afterward, they both collapsed against the pillows trying to catch their breath.

"That was..." she started.

"Yeah, I know. Beyond incredible," he finished as he laced their fingers together. Everything about this woman turned him on, and he wouldn't mind staying this way for the rest of the day. He wondered what Troy and Kyle would do if he backed out of their excursion.

"What are you thinking about?"

He laughed softly. "I was trying to come up with an excuse to back out on my friends."

"I don't think that's a good idea."

He rolled his head in her direction. "Tired of my company already?"

"Not at all. I was thinking you just got out of the doghouse for being a bad friend. It would be a shame for you to be back in so soon."

Damian stared at her in disbelief, then laughed heartily. Soon they were both laughing hard. "Wow. I don't know if

I should be offended or not. I've never been with a woman who *wanted* me to go out with the guys."

Still chuckling, she said, "Don't be. I just happen to think good friends are hard to come by, and it's important to spend time with them when you can."

He quieted, thinking about her words. "Yeah. I agree. So do you plan to go ashore?"

"Yes. Janae and Terrence are making an appearance, and we're all going to lunch. Beyond that, I have no idea what we're doing."

He sat up and swung his legs over the side of the bed. "I guess I should probably get moving." He stood, retrieved his clothes and dressed quickly. He would shower once he got back to his room. But first he glanced back at Karen spread out on the bed looking sexy as hell—wild hair, kiss-swollen lips—with the sheet barely covering her body. She made an alluring picture. It was all he could do not to climb back into that bed.

She obviously interpreted his thoughts because she said, "Stop looking at me like that and go meet your friends."

Busted, he dropped his head. He leaned down and kissed her. "I'll see you tonight, sweetheart."

She gave him a tiny wave and smiled. "Bye. Have fun."

He stood there a minute longer, willing his feet to move. Finally, he forced himself to leave. Giving her one last look, he reluctantly opened the door and left with every detail about her imprinted on his brain.

Damian strolled down the corridor toward the elevator. He smiled. Yeah, he would enjoy the day with his friends, but his night—that would belong to Karen.

Chapter 7

"I wasn't sure you'd show up," Troy said when Damian set his plate on the table and lowered himself into the chair across from Troy.

"Believe me, I thought about canceling," Damian muttered, spreading strawberry jam on his biscuit. In his mind, he replayed last night and this morning. His groin throbbed in remembrance of Karen riding him. Kyle's laughter broke into his thoughts.

"You're daydreaming, bro. It must have been a helluva night."

"It was." They ate in silence for a few minutes.

"You're really feeling Karen?" Troy asked, forking up some scrambled eggs on his plate.

"I like her."

Troy raised an eyebrow. "You like her? That's it? As much time as you're spending with her, that's all you're gonna say?"

Damian shrugged. "It's only been a couple of days, so yeah, that's all I'm saying." He wasn't ready to share his feelings because he didn't quite understand them himself. They stared at him. "What?"

Kyle drained his glass of orange juice and shook his head. "You must really like her if you were thinking about canceling." He cocked his head to the side. "Out of curiosity, what made you decide not to cancel?"

"Karen. She said good friends are hard to come by and that I should take advantage of the time."

"Sounds like a wise woman." They finished breakfast, and Kyle checked his watch. "We should get going."

They all rose from the table and grabbed their backpacks. "You're still not telling me what we're doing?" Damian asked.

"We're gonna have some fun. That's all you need to know." Troy clapped him on the shoulder. "It'll be like old times when we used to go hiking or motorcycle riding."

Ten minutes later, the three men headed into town. They stopped to do a short tour of the Atlantis Resort and ended up engaging in a car race on the Raceway, which Kyle won and couldn't stop bragging about.

"It was only one race, and you *barely* won," Damian said.

"The fact remains, I won. I knew that tactical driving course would come in handy someday." Kyle was a former police detective.

"That wasn't tactical driving. That was cheating. If you hadn't cut me off, I would've won."

Kyle laughed. "Like I said, *tactical* driving."

"Whatever," Damian muttered. "What else are we doing?"

"We're taking a short hop over to one of the private islands to do some snorkeling," Troy answered.

They were shuttled to the dock area, where Troy had chartered a boat. The ride lasted less than an hour, and Damian could only stare at the island's lush beauty—endless blue sky, powder-white sand and warm turquoise water. "This is amazing. How did you guys find out about this place?"

"My old buddy from the force, Joshua, told us about it," Kyle answered. "He came with us four years ago. Troy and I come back every time we cruise this way." He gestured around. "See all this beauty you've been missing?"

He surveyed the area again. "Yeah." Four years ago would have been the first time they invited him to join them on the cruise. Back then nothing could pull him out of the deep funk he'd been in. The only thing he had wanted was to make it through the day.

Troy seemed to sense what was going though his head. "You're here now, so let's have some fun."

They headed over to one of the three buildings on the beach, where they were outfitted with snorkeling equipment. For the next two hours, they explored the depths of crystal-clear waters and saw a variety of plant and animal life. Once they finished, the three men returned the equipment, showered and ate lunch at the small beachfront grill. There were about a dozen people inside, so it didn't take long to get their food. Damian took his friends' suggestion and ordered the steamed fish, baked macaroni and cheese, and potato salad. Troy ordered a side of johnnycake— a slightly sweet flavored bread. Lifting their glasses of planter's punch, they toasted to friendship and dug in.

"Oh," Damian said, "this is good."

"Told you," Troy said around a mouthful of macaroni and cheese. "This mac and cheese is better than my mama's." He glanced up and pointed his fork at Damian and Kyle. "And if either one of you two clowns mentions that to her, I'll kick your asses."

Damian grinned. "Man, I'm three inches taller, outweigh you by a good thirty pounds and, unlike you, work out regularly. It'll be no contest."

"Hell, I'll just shoot you," Kyle tossed out with a shrug.

They looked at each other and laughed. The trash-talking continued throughout the meal, and Damian realized how much he had missed hanging out with his friends. He downed the last of his drink, wiped his mouth and tossed the napkin on his empty plate. Leaning back in the chair, he groaned. "I haven't eaten like this in ages."

"Me, either," Kyle said. "Let's snag one of those loungers or a hammock and let this food digest."

The men dragged themselves over beneath large palm trees. Troy collapsed onto a lounger, while Damian and Kyle chose hammocks. The temperatures hovered near eighty, and the peaceful surroundings immediately relaxed Damian. His mind automatically shifted to Karen. He wondered whether she was still on the island or back on the ship. He continued to be in awe of their chemistry in and out of bed. He would love to have her next to him cuddled in the hammock. His eyes slid closed, and with a smile on his face, he drifted off.

Troy's voice startled him and interrupted an incredible dream he was having about Karen.

"Damian. Wake up."

His eyes popped open, and he ran a hand over his face. "What time is it?"

"Five."

He sat up so quickly he almost tumbled out of the hammock. Coming to his feet, he glared at Troy and Kyle. *"What?"* His heart started to pound in alarm. "The ship is supposed to leave at five."

Kyle climbed out of the hammock near him, yawned and stretched. "We know. We're staying overnight and catching up with the ship tomorrow in Key West."

Damian cursed. "Why didn't you tell me that?" he roared.

"Man, calm down. We just wanted you to experience a little Caribbean nightlife before we head back," Kyle said.

Troy frowned. "We didn't think it would be a big deal."

"Well, it is a big deal," Damian said through clenched teeth. "I told Karen we'd have dinner tonight." He paced back and forth, imagining what kinds of thoughts would run through her mind when he didn't show up at her door as promised. He stopped pacing, dropped down in a nearby lounger and cradled his head in his palms. All his plans… gone.

"Sorry, man. We didn't know," Troy said softly, regret coloring his words.

Damian met Troy's gaze and heaved a deep sigh. "I know."

"I'll be happy to talk to Karen when we get back tomorrow and tell her it was our fault," Kyle added.

A member of the crew came over to let them know it was time to leave. Collecting their belongings, they followed the man back to the boat, boarded and made the short trip in silence. Then they hailed a taxi to transport them to the hotel where they would spend the night. The lavish hotel had every amenity imaginable, along with activities for the single crowd unmatched by any other hotel. However, the only thing on Damian's mind was Karen and how he would convince her to continue what they had started beyond the cruise.

Karen slept for another hour after Damian left, then got up and took a long soak in the Jacuzzi. Her muscles were a little sore from the intense workout they'd had. She leaned her head against the towel she'd rolled up and relaxed under the powerful jets.

A smile played around the corners of her mouth. The man knew his way around a woman's body, and she was glad to be on the receiving end. She remembered him saying it had been a while since he was intimate with a woman and briefly wondered why. Had he gotten his heart broken, too? Although they were only enjoying each other's company for the duration of the cruise, she wouldn't mind keeping in touch with him. They seemed to have several things in common, and most important, he hadn't ridiculed her career choice. Karen didn't know whether he was on the same page, but she thought she might casually bring it up over dinner this evening.

She completed her bath, dressed and went to meet her friends. Only Donovan and Terrence's two other friends, Audrey and Brad, had arrived at the designated meeting spot.

"What's up, Karen?" Donovan said, leaning down to kiss her cheek.

"Hey, Donovan."

"Terrence and Janae are going to be a few minutes late."

"Surprise, surprise," she said with a laugh. She spoke to Audrey and Brad. "Are you guys enjoying the cruise?"

"Most definitely." Audrey stared at her husband, her blue eyes shining with love. Brad brushed his hand across her cheek and placed a tender kiss on her lips.

"All right, you two, knock it off," Donovan muttered. "You're as bad as Terrence and Janae."

Karen laughed, but inside she wished a man looked at her with the love Brad had for Audrey. The look in Damian's eyes when he wiped her tears at last night's show surfaced in her mind. For a split second, she felt something, thought she saw something other than their obvious physical attraction. *Probably just my imagination and wishful thinking.* Devin's voice broke into her thoughts.

"Morning, everybody." There was another round of greetings. "I guess we're waiting for the newlyweds, *again*?"

"Yep," she said. The group chatted amiably for several minutes before Karen spotted Janae and Terrence approaching. "It's about time."

"Sorry. We sort of lost track of time," Terrence said with a sheepish grin.

Karen met Janae's smiling face and nodded knowingly. "Uh-huh."

"Now that Mr. and Mrs. Campbell have graced us with their presence, let's get this party started," Donovan said.

Karen took pictures as they walked through the Welcome Center to downtown Nassau. "The kids are going to love these photos." They entered a small shop.

"Girl, I know. Are you getting any souvenirs?" Janae asked.

She nodded. "I picked up something for them in Jamaica."

"You bought something for all thirty-four students?"

"I did. I have such a good class this year. They've been working hard, and their test scores show it. So I decided to reward them."

"And *that's* why you're the favorite teacher at the school…and why Nikki is always trying to one-up you."

"Please don't remind me about that woman." Nikki Fleming taught another fourth-grade class, and for the past two years had tried to undermine Karen at every turn. If Karen suggested a strategy to improve test scores or ways to engage the students, Nikki made it her business to come up with a reason why it couldn't work. "I don't know what her problem is. She's gotten even worse this year, if that's possible."

"Maybe she'll get an offer to teach in another state," Janae said wryly.

"I should be so lucky. I'd settle for one in another district," she said, following the group out of the crowded shop and into another one.

In the fourth shop, she found a cute wrap skirt and a T-shirt. She conversed with Janae and Audrey, but her mind kept straying to Damian and secretly hoping she would run into him while on the island. They had lunch in a restaurant recommended by Donovan and Terrence that served local specialties. Karen ate conch fritters, cracked lobster, potato salad and plantains, and washed it all down with a mango daiquiri.

"I'm so full. I think I need a nap now," she said with a groan.

Audrey laughed. "I hear you." She pointed to the guys, who were still stuffing their faces. "I don't know how they eat all this food."

"If I ate like that for just one day, I'd gain ten pounds," Janae said.

"Amen, sister." Karen and Janae raised their hands for a high five, and all three women fell out laughing.

"It's a good thing there are only two more nights on this cruise. Otherwise I might be needing a new wardrobe," Audrey said. "Hmm…"

"You ain't said nothing but a word, Audrey. All I need is an excuse. This one here," she added, eyeing Janae, "is no fun when it comes to shopping."

Janae rolled her eyes. "Please. That's because you get out of control whenever we go shopping. Five hours in a mall is just plain crazy."

"Five hours of nothing but shopping is like pure heaven," Audrey said, sighing wistfully. "Karen, let me know the next time you come to LA. Girl, I know all the great shopping spots—sales like you wouldn't believe."

Karen rubbed her hands together with glee. "Count me in."

"I'll pass," Janae said.

"Oh, come on, Janae," Karen pleaded. "It'll be so much fun."

"I don't think so."

"Tell you what. Karen, you and I can swing by and pick her up halfway through the day. We'll even feed her first."

"Audrey, two hours of shopping is my limit." Janae held up two fingers. *"Two."*

"Yes!" Karen tapped her chin thoughtfully. "I need to check my calendar to see which weekend I can fly down."

Once the guys finished eating, everyone headed over to

the beach. Audrey and Brad excused themselves and left to take a walk. A group of fans recognized Terrence, and he stopped to sign autographs with Donovan and Devin playing bodyguard.

Janae pulled Karen off to the side. "So how are things going with Damian?"

"Fine, I guess." Karen didn't know how to describe her feelings toward Damian. This was supposed to be nothing more than enjoying the company of a nice guy while on the cruise. Instead her feelings had taken on a life of their own.

"What does that mean?"

"I don't know. He's a really nice guy, and I like him."

"That's a good thing."

"I didn't count on liking him this much. He's an absolute gentleman, a great conversationalist, and makes me lose my mind with his kisses."

Janae raised an eyebrow. "That good, huh?"

"Girl, yes. He is beyond amazing. Said it had been a while since he'd been with a woman, but if that's his definition of being out of practice…"

"Sounds like you two hit it off pretty well. Might be something worth exploring."

Karen frowned. "I don't think so. I don't even know where the man lives."

"You do realize this is the twenty-first century. There's email, texting, Skype—"

"Ha-ha, Ms. Smarty-Pants. I know that." She shrugged. "But it's not something we've talked about. For all I know, he may not want anything past this week."

"Well, you never know unless you ask."

"True." Admittedly, Karen would like to see where things could go between them, but she didn't want to set herself up for disappointment.

They hung out at the beach for a while longer and then

headed back to the ship to give Terrence time to prepare for his Q & A session.

Later, after the session, Karen stood in line with the others to purchase and get her CD signed. Donovan told her she didn't have to wait, but she didn't feel right about cutting the line. To her surprise, Terrence told her the CD was on the house.

He handed her a CD, stood to take a picture with her and whispered, "I already signed this special one for you. I'll always be grateful to you for bringing Janae to the concert. I can't imagine my life without her. If you ever need anything, let me know."

She hugged him. "Aw, you're so sweet. Tell you what, if I get lucky enough to meet a special guy, you sing at my wedding and we'll call it even."

"Deal." He grinned. "I saw the guy you were with. Should I be getting a song ready?"

Karen laughed. "You might want to hold off on that. Like I told your wife, I have no idea where the man lives."

"Janae and I started as a long-distance relationship," he pointed out.

She ignored his comment. "You have a long line of people waiting."

He chuckled. "Okay. I can take a hint. See you later. We're celebrating tomorrow night. Janae will fill you in."

"All right."

Karen went back to her room and took a short nap. Eating all that good food and being in the sun had drained her. When she woke up, she still had a couple of hours before dinner with Damian. Picking up her novel off the nightstand, she slid the balcony door open and stepped outside. She stared out over the water as the boat moved farther away from Nassau.

They had one last stop in Key West tomorrow before reaching Miami the following day. The week seemed to have flown by and went much better than she had anticipated. Nowhere in her wildest dreams did she ever think she'd meet a man like Damian. Would he want to continue what they had started or relegate her to his past? Sure, they had several things in common and got along great in and out of bed, but would that be enough?

She released a heavy sigh. Everything was going great until things moved past the physical to the emotional. *And this is why I shouldn't let my feelings get involved.* Karen lowered herself into one of the cushioned chairs and opened the book. She tried concentrating on the words, but her mind kept wandering to dinner with Damian. After sitting there for nearly an hour, she closed the book, got to her feet and went inside to shower. She dressed, styled her hair and applied light makeup. The closer it got to seven, the more nervous she became.

When seven o'clock came and went, her nervousness turned to concern. The phone rang and she snatched it up, hoping it was Damian.

"Hey, girl," Janae said when Karen answered.

"Hey."

"I wanted to let you know that some of Terrence's musician friends are throwing us a party tomorrow night. It's going to be in the Sapphire Room again at eight. You're welcome to bring Damian. Are you guys getting together tonight?"

"We were supposed to go to dinner, but I haven't heard from him."

"What time was dinner?"

"Half an hour ago."

"Maybe he lost track of time with his friends. I'm sure he'll be there."

"Maybe." But she wasn't convinced.

"Well, I'll let you go in case he's trying to call. I'll see you tomorrow."

"All right." Karen placed the phone in the cradle.

As the minutes and hours ticked off, she realized Damian wasn't coming. She never thought he'd be the type of man to do something like this, but she was wrong. Again. She changed into her pajamas and crawled into bed, vowing not to let her guard down ever again.

Chapter 8

Damian could hear the music and laughter floating through the open French doors leading to his balcony. Kyle and Troy had tried to get him to join them, but he couldn't be bothered. What he wanted was to be with Karen. He rose from the chair he had been sitting in for the past hour and stepped out onto the balcony. Folding his arms across his chest, he tilted his head back and closed his eyes. He had only come on the cruise to get his friends off his back. He never intended to meet a woman, much less form an instant connection with one—a connection that he seemed to have no control over. Did she feel it, as well?

Tonight he had planned to fill in all the gaps, starting with her last name and where she lived. He shook his head, not believing he hadn't even asked her last name. Damian didn't care where she lived, as long as she agreed to keep seeing him. He wanted to tell her that he shared her passion for teaching and the joy of seeing new minds come alive. He still would…if he got the chance. Would she accept his apology? Even if she did, it was no guarantee she'd want to continue what they had started. A knock on the door interrupted his thoughts. He went back inside, crossed the spacious suite and opened the door to find Troy and Kyle standing there. Damian stepped back and waved them in.

"What are you guys doing here? I thought you'd be well into the night action by now."

"Yeah. Me, too," Kyle said. "But it's hard to have a good

time knowing you're up here miserable." He dropped down on a sofa, stretched out and flung an arm across his face.

Troy took a seat in a chair, and Damian sat across from him in a matching one. "I feel bad about making you miss your dinner with Karen. To make it up to you, I chartered a seaplane for tomorrow."

"I'll pitch in for the cost," Damian said.

Troy waved him off. "Nah, man. Don't worry about it since it was our fault. We should've asked you if you had plans, knowing how much time you two have been spending together."

"Is this thing serious between you two?" Kyle asked.

"I can't say it's serious, but I feel something for her I've never felt with any other woman."

Kyle brought his arm down and rolled his head in Damian's direction. "Even Joyce?"

Damian hesitated before answering quietly, "Yes." He'd asked himself the question and knew the answer, but saying the word out loud made him feel as though he was betraying Joyce.

Troy regarded him for a moment. "We figured as much."

"What does that mean?"

"Damian, we never thought…"

"Thought what?" Damian asked when Troy trailed off.

"We always wondered whether Joyce was the right woman for you. And after seeing you with Karen—"

Damian jumped up from the chair. "What the hell does that mean?"

"It means," Kyle started, coming to a sitting position, "that you and Joyce seemed more like best friends than lovers."

"Are you saying I didn't love my *wife*?" Damian exploded.

Kyle blew out a harsh breath. "Calm down, man. No,

that's not what I'm saying. Can you sit down, please? I'm getting a crick in my neck."

He plopped his six-foot-four-inch frame in the chair, crossed his arms and glared at Kyle.

"I know you loved Joyce, but were you *in* love with her—that deep, passionate kind of love that makes you lose your mind?"

Damian didn't answer. He and Joyce had shared a close friendship and trusted each other. And there were other reasons that factored into their marriage—reasons he'd never shared with anyone. No, they didn't have a passionate love, but he did love her.

"It's the kind of love that when you look at her, your only thought is how much you want to be with her."

"Sort of like the way you look at Karen," Troy said.

Damian frowned. "What, you're a mind reader now?"

"We've known each other for over twenty years. I'm sure you'd be able to see the same thing in Kyle or me. Look, Damian, Joyce was a sweet girl, and we all loved her, but it seemed as if you stopped living once you two married."

"We didn't expect you to hang out with us like you had before, but you never accepted the invitations even when Joyce was invited," Kyle added. "We don't want to see the same thing happen again."

He had never stopped to think about how cut off they'd been from life. His wife hadn't been much of a people person, and he hadn't wanted her to be uncomfortable, so he started declining invitations from his friends and family until, gradually, the invitations stopped. Damian remembered his own mother mentioning something similar a time or two.

"And you think that if I'm with Karen, I'll do the same thing again." He divided his gaze between the two men. Neither answered, but their expressions told all, and he felt his anger rising. "First of all, you're acting like I'm planning to get married right now, which I'm not. Second, Karen and Joyce are two different women."

"Look, we're not trying to upset you," Troy said. "But we're brothers. And when one of us is hurting, it affects us all. We've been worried about you, man. This week is the first time in a long while that you've been relaxed and almost happy like you used to be. I can't even imagine how hard it was to lose Joyce. But I just don't want you to go back to being the same way after this week is over."

Damian sat quietly as he digested Troy's words. Yeah, it had been hard, but honestly over the past few months, he'd begun to feel restless, as though he was ready to move on. He'd even gone on dates, but hadn't found a woman who stirred his interest. Until now.

"You used to be the one we could always count on for a good laugh." Kyle chuckled, as if remembering.

"You guys have always had my back. Though I may not have said it lately, I do appreciate it." Damian shook his head. "Not sure how much I appreciate all this advice, though," he said wryly.

"Hey, that's what friends and *brothers* do," Kyle said pointedly.

Damian nodded. "I realized this week that I miss having fun," he confessed. "I can't go back to being alone all the time."

"What if things don't work out with Karen?"

Once again, the thought of not being able to give their relationship a chance didn't sit well with him. "Even if they don't, I'm going to try to get out more."

"My boy is back!"

"Shut up, Kyle." But Damian was grinning as he said it. The three friends spent the evening catching up and reminiscing about old times. Damian enjoyed himself but anxiously awaited morning so he could get back to the ship…and Karen.

As soon as he'd boarded the ship the next day, Damian went to Karen's room but got no answer. He spent more than an hour searching the deck and various places for her, before concluding that she might have gone ashore. His friends agreed and convinced Damian to have lunch and wait for the ship to leave before resuming his search. When the ship pulled out of the dock, Damian strode urgently down the hallway toward her room, hoping to catch her before dinner. He stopped at her door and knocked. When she didn't answer, he knocked again.

"Karen? It's Damian."

He needed to find her and explain. Damian knew she was probably upset with him and wondered if she was in the room and refusing to answer. No. She wasn't that kind of person. An elderly couple stopped at the room across from hers, and the man eyed Damian warily. Moving away from the door, Damian trudged back the way he had come and took the elevator to the main dining restaurant and started his search again.

There had to be more than a thousand people on this cruise. Everyone seemed to be out milling around and enjoying their last night, which made looking for Karen more difficult. He ended up back on the deck staring out over the water, thinking about what would happen when he found Karen. In a perfect world, they'd exchange personal information and then… Realistically, life never went according to plan, and he had to wrap his mind around the possibility that she'd say no. However, the chemistry between them remained strong, and he'd use that as his starting point. But he had to find her first.

It was nearly midnight when Damian decided to try

knocking on Karen's door again. At the last moment, he scribbled a note, leaving his number and asking her to wait for him in the morning before disembarking, just in case she hadn't returned. He took the elevator to her deck and moved quickly down the corridor.

He stopped at her door and took a deep breath. Raising his hand, he knocked softly. No answer. He knocked harder and called out to her.

"It's a little late to be going around knocking on folks' doors, don't you think, son?"

Damian spun around to find the elderly gentleman he'd seen earlier that evening—the last time Damian came to the door—standing in his doorway wearing a pair of striped flannel pajamas.

"Either the young lady isn't in, or she's sending you a message."

Damian lowered his head in embarrassment. "I apologize for disturbing you, sir."

The man regarded him silently and nodded. He smiled knowingly and said, "I hope things turn out for you."

"So do I," he said. "Again, my apologies."

The man nodded once more and closed his door softly.

Damian pulled the note out of his pocket, slid it under the door, then made his way back to his room to pack. He tossed and turned for hours, finally drifting off near dawn. It seemed as if he had just closed his eyes when a loud bang next door startled him. He groaned and glanced over at the clock. *Eight*. He cursed under his breath and jumped off the bed. Snatching back the curtains, he saw buildings and realized they were pulling into port.

He quickly showered and dressed. Praying she hadn't left, he hurried to Karen's room. His anxiety mounted as two elevators passed because they were full. When he finally got to her room, Damian's heart nearly stopped. The door stood open, and the housekeeper's cart blocked the entry. *I'm too late.* He peeked in the room, knowing she was gone, but wanting to be wrong.

Sighing heavily, he trudged to his room. Kyle and Troy stepped out into the hall as he reached the door. Before they could ask, Damian shook his head, opened the door and grabbed his bags.

"Let's go." He walked off.

They disembarked and took a shuttle to the airport. After they arrived and went through security, Damian dropped into a chair to wait. Thankfully they had a morning flight, as he had no desire to sit around for hours. When the time came, he boarded the plane, settled into the seat and closed his eyes.

Had Karen gotten the note? Or was she—as the gentleman last night put it—sending him a message? The whys and what-ifs continued to attack him, and as the plane lifted off, he was left with wondering, once again, what could have been.

Chapter 9

Karen received a warm welcome back when she walked through the school office early Monday morning and her students greeted her with squeals, laughter and hugs. It was just the lift she needed after spending another restless night thinking about Damian. Last night, when she reached into the tote bag and took out the two books, the photo of her and Damian from Dunn's River Falls slipped out. She had lingered over every detail of his face and body—wet, sun-browned, smooth skin with those swim trunks plastered against him, hazel eyes and that killer smile.

Why couldn't she have stuck to her promise to stay away from men? They only brought on heartaches and headaches. Karen couldn't bring herself to throw the picture out and, after much inner debate, had placed it in the nightstand drawer. As much as she wanted to think of Damian as a fling, she knew, in those few short days, he had become more. But she'd never see him again and prayed his memory would fade soon.

Bringing herself back to the present, she hugged as many students as she could. "Okay. Let's line up." The students quickly got in line, and she led them to the classroom.

Karen took care of attendance and lunch count, then went over the daily schedule.

"Ms. Morris?" a student called. "Did you take any pictures?"

"Yes. As soon as everyone is quiet, I'll show you a few,

and then we'll have journal writing." She had downloaded some of the pictures onto a flash drive. Once the students settled, she turned the lights off and projected the pictures she'd taken onto the screen. They oohed and aahed as each picture filled the screen. Afterward, she turned the lights back on. "All right. Today in your journals I want you to tell me about your favorite vacation. Remember to do your best writing—letters on the line, spaces between words and correct capitalization and punctuation."

The day went by in a blur. She waited until the students were ready to leave before handing out the souvenirs. By the time the last student left, Karen was exhausted but glad to be back doing what she loved. She was putting the last of the books on a shelf when she heard a voice behind her.

"Hey, Karen."

"Hey, Melissa." Melissa Tucker was the school psychologist. Karen often helped her lead the conflict management group.

"Girl, I've been waiting all day to talk to you. I want to hear about that cruise." She took a seat on the edge of a desk.

Karen told her all about the wedding, Jamaica and the Bahamas.

"That sounds heavenly. So, did you meet any hot guys while you were there?" she asked slyly.

"I was there to see my best friend get married and relax, not meet guys." Karen walked over, sat at her desk and shut down her computer. The last thing she wanted was a reminder of the *hot guy* she had met.

Melissa came and stood in front of the desk, scrutinizing Karen with an intensity that almost made her squirm in the chair. She braced both hands on the desk. "Oh, my goodness! You met somebody, didn't you?"

"I just told you—"

"Please. It's written all over your face. Now spill it."

Karen sighed heavily. "His name is—well, *was* Damian."

"Ooh, does he look as fine as that name suggests?" Melissa asked with a grin.

"Finer," she admitted. She told Melissa how she'd met Damian, about the time they spent in Jamaica and their subsequent night together.

"Sounds like you had a great time with a great guy."

"Yeah, that's what I thought, too…until he stood me up and went MIA." She shrugged. "Anyway, it's no big deal. I'll probably never see him again, and we had fun while it lasted. He was just someone to pass the time with on the cruise, that's all."

"Well, at least you weren't bored," Melissa said with a laugh.

Karen's mind traveled back to dancing in the club, climbing the falls and snuggling in Damian's arms. "No, not at all." She waved a hand. "Enough of that. What's going on?"

"I know you heard about Priscilla. It's such a shame about her husband." Priscilla Mitchell, the school principal, had been absent the two days before Karen left for Janae's wedding, and suddenly retired the following week after her husband's involvement in a head-on collision. He would need full-time care for the foreseeable future.

"I heard, and it is. I'm going to miss her. She took me under her wing when I first came here." Karen had a special place in her heart for the woman who had mentored her when Karen started teaching eight years ago. They had developed a natural rapport, and the woman became a surrogate mother to Karen.

Melissa angled her head thoughtfully and wagged a finger at Karen. "You should think about applying for the position. They're going to fill it pretty quickly, I'm sure.

Until then, we're sharing a vice principal from one of the middle schools."

"What? I don't know," Karen said skeptically.

"Why not? You have your master's, and your concentration is in administration. You also have your counseling certificate. I think you'd be great."

"Hmm. Maybe." She had been thinking about going the administrative route. This might be the opportunity she was looking for. She unlocked a drawer, pulled out her purse, slung it over her shoulder and stood. "I'll think about it. Right now I'm going home. It's been a long day."

"I hear you. I'll be right behind you. Oh, I almost forgot, you and I will be going to a safety training next month."

"Is this something new?" Karen asked as they walked toward the front office.

"It's a two-day train-the-trainer type of thing. With all the shootings and mess going on in the schools, Priscilla wanted to make sure we have the best emergency preparedness program available. Plus, a lot of our stuff is really outdated. She heard about the company from her sister, who lives in Georgia. So she asked the superintendent about it, and he approved it. There'll be two people from each school in the district to serve as first responders or points of contact." She leaned closer and lowered her voice to a whisper. "Nikki was *not* happy when she wasn't chosen. She was even more pissed when Priscilla chose you, especially since you were on the cruise."

Karen shook her head. "I don't know why that woman has it in for me. I've never done anything to her."

"Except be a great teacher," Melissa said.

Karen rolled her eyes. "Isn't that supposed to be the goal of all teachers?"

"One would think so."

Not wanting to discuss Nikki Fleming further, Karen

returned to their previous conversation. "When is the training again?"

"Monday and Tuesday of the week before Thanksgiving. But they'll be coming back to spend about a week here doing assemblies for the kids and parents, checking out our current plan and helping to revamp it if necessary. You and I will work with them."

"What about my class?"

"From what I understand, most of the meetings will be before or after school."

"Great. There goes my free time."

"Hey, if we're lucky, at least one of the trainers from DKT Safety Consultants will be fine and sexy, as opposed to old and wrinkled and smelling like Bengay." Melissa wrinkled her nose.

Karen laughed. "Only you, Melissa. Only you." In her mind, old was safer. She didn't need fine and sexy.

"What? I need some male stimulation in my life. It's been too long. And you never know, one of them might help you get over your cruise-ship fling."

She grunted. "No, thanks. I'll pass." Besides, it would take *some* man to help her get over Damian.

Damian sat in his office staring out the window. He had been back to work a week, and memories of Karen plagued him day and night. No matter who he was talking to or what he was doing, visions of her danced around the edges of his mind. At night when he closed his eyes, he could see her face and hear her laughter. And sometimes he'd swear he could smell her intoxicating fragrance. He tried working out at the gym—pushing himself far beyond his limits—thinking if he were tired enough, he'd be able to sleep. Damian's old sleeping patterns had returned, and he found himself up prowling half the night.

Several times over the week he asked himself why he

hadn't camped out at her door instead of leaving a note. But he knew the answer. He didn't want to risk her rejection. More than once, he wondered whether they kept missing each other or if she had chosen not to answer her door, as well as not to respond to his note. What if she hadn't felt the connection as deeply as he had, or worse, she'd moved on? Somehow, in those few short days, Karen had made an impact on him. On his heart. And he had no idea how to deal with that, especially since there was the possibility that he would never see her again. Again he asked himself, why her? Why now? And would their paths ever cross again? Damian rotated his chair toward the door upon hearing a knock.

"What's up, Kyle?"

Kyle handed him a sheet of paper. "Here's the schedule for November and December. There's going to be a little more back-and-forth because of the holidays."

Damian accepted and scanned the sheet. "California?"

Kyle smiled. "Yep. West Coast. We're branching out. The first week and a half we'll be in LA and San Diego— just a couple of schools and a company wanting emergency preparedness training."

Damian glanced back at the sheet. "Looks like we're going to be spending more time in the Bay Area." There were schools in Oakland, San Francisco and San Jose. Some wanted one- or two-day train-the-trainer workshops, and others wanted that in addition to a full-scale school site overhaul. "We start there before Thanksgiving and go back in December," he murmured.

"I haven't been to Cali in a while. We'll have to schedule some fun time."

"I'm all for a change of scenery." Damian was tired of looking at the same walls every day. Although they wouldn't leave for another three weeks, maybe the trip would help him forget Karen.

"How've you been since we've been back? Are you still thinking about Karen?"

"Yeah, man. I can't get her off my mind. I don't know… there's just something about her."

"What's her last name?"

"I have no idea."

Kyle gave a shout of laughter. "What do you mean you don't know? You spent what…two, three days together, and you don't know her last name?"

"I know it sounds crazy, but we seemed to talk about everything except ourselves. I don't even know where she's from or where she lives." He gave Kyle a sidelong glance. "You used to be a detective. Can't you use some of that legendary expertise I keep hearing about to help me out?"

Kyle leaned against the door frame and folded his arms across his chest. "A detective…yes. God…no. Last time I checked, He was the only one who's all-knowing. Now, if you had a last name, and possibly the state, I may have been able to help you out." He chuckled. "Man, how could you not get the woman's last name? That's like Dating 101."

"At first, it didn't matter—you know, dinner and nice conversation." He hadn't planned on anything past the first night, didn't count on the explosive chemistry between them or the passion she ignited in him.

"Obviously, you didn't count on falling for Karen," Kyle said, reading Damian's mind.

"No. I didn't."

"Maybe this was a sign that you're ready for love again." He pushed off the wall. "See you later."

"Later."

Damian stayed way past closing. He made it home in record time, parked in the garage and entered the house, not bothering to turn on the lights. He knew every square inch with his eyes closed. His footsteps echoed loudly on the wooden floors in the otherwise silent space. In his upstairs bedroom, Damian shrugged out of his jacket and tossed it on a chair. He dropped down heavily on the side of the bed and removed his shoes.

His gaze strayed to the nightstand, where he had placed the photo of him and Karen taken in front of the falls. They looked good together. He picked it up, and his body automatically reacted as he remembered the heated kisses they'd shared while they climbed, opening a floodgate of memories. This time, instead of fighting them, he let them come—the texture of her velvety smooth skin beneath his hands, the sweetness of her kiss as their tongues danced and the scorching passion they shared that left him wanting more.

But it wasn't only about the physical connection. She stimulated him intellectually and enjoyed some of the same things he did. He studied the picture. He thought keeping busy would help him forget her, but Karen wasn't the type of woman a man could easily forget. Truth be told, he didn't want to. Although he had no idea how he would accomplish it, Damian hoped to find her again.

The next three weeks seemed to crawl by, and Damian was more than ready for the trip when the day came. As he packed, the phone rang and he activated the speaker on the cordless phone.

"Do you have me on that speaker, Damian?" his mother asked when he answered.

He sighed. "Yes, Mom. I have to pack, and it's easier than me trying to hold the phone."

"I hate that thing," she muttered.

He stifled a groan. He loved his mother, but he didn't have time for this today. He needed to be at the airport in two hours. "I know, Mom. What's going on?"

"Nothing. You've been back from that cruise over three

weeks. I thought you would've called me by now to tell me about it. Well?"

"Well, what?" he asked as he stuffed socks and underwear in the suitcase.

"Did you enjoy yourself?" she asked with an impatient sigh.

Loaded question. "It was fine." He went to the closet, took down four suits and put them in his garment bag.

"Damian, are you still there?"

"I'm here, Mom."

"I didn't hear you."

"I said it was fine. Great music and food, beautiful islands." And one extraordinary woman.

"Sounds like fun. Did you meet any nice girls? I'm sure there were plenty available."

Before he could fix his mouth to lie, "yes" tumbled out. He slapped a hand across his forehead.

"Really?" she asked excitedly. "What's her name, and when will I get to meet her?"

Damian sat down on the bed and picked up the phone, deactivating the speaker. "Her name is Karen, and probably never."

"Oh, that's too bad. I was hoping you'd find someone. I want you to be happy. You deserve to fall in love."

"What does that mean?" When she hesitated, he said, "Mom, what are you saying?"

"I'm simply saying I want you to find someone special."

"What about Joyce? Are you saying I wasn't in love?"

"No, honey. Joyce was a wonderful girl. I loved her like a daughter, but I just want you to be happy."

"Thanks, Mom." First his friends, and now his mother.

She hesitated. "Sweetheart, I know all about that promise you made to Joyce's grandmother."

His stomach dropped. He had never told anyone about that.

"If she wanted to interfere in her granddaughter's life,

that was her prerogative, but I made sure Lillian knew, in explicit detail, how I felt about her interfering in my son's life. Meddling old biddy," she grumbled. "I was two seconds from stopping that wedding. You and Joyce both deserved to find that special someone, and Lillian, with her selfish and manipulative ways, messed that up."

Joyce's grandmother had been diagnosed with terminal cancer and only had a few months to live. She extracted a promise from Damian to look out for Joyce, saying she could go to her grave a happy woman knowing her granddaughter would be taken care of. He knew what the woman was asking. Initially, he had no intention of being manipulated into marriage, but her rapid decline and the sadness in Joyce's eyes pushed him over the edge. It wasn't as if he and Joyce didn't get along. They were best friends, and he loved her. "I can't believe you knew all this time and never said anything. So what made you change your mind about stopping the wedding?"

"Your father. He reminded me that you were a grown man and could make your own decisions. That we raised you to be God-fearing, respectful and honorable, and you were all of those things."

"Remind me to give Dad a big hug the next time I come to visit. Mom, I don't want you to think that I wasn't happy with Joyce. I was. I loved her."

"I know, and I'm glad. Do you think you'll ever want to try marriage again?"

"For a long time I didn't, but now…"

"Does this have anything to do with the woman you met on the cruise?"

"Yes." He told her about the days he spent with Karen, how much he enjoyed being with her and about the mishap. "She probably thinks I stood her up, and I didn't get a chance to tell her what happened."

"Well, I'm sure if you gave her a call, she'd be willing to listen."

"I don't have her number. We sort of never got around to last names and exchanging personal information. I had planned to do all that at dinner."

She laughed. "No last name and no phone number? That must have been *some* attraction."

He cleared his throat. "Um…Mom, I need to get going."

Still chuckling, she said, "Okay. Keep me posted on any potential daughters-in-law. I need some grandchildren. How long are you going to be gone?"

It was definitely time to hang up. "Close to three weeks. I'll be home for Thanksgiving, then head west again for another two or three weeks. I'll call you when I get back."

"All right. Give my love to Kyle and Troy, and you boys be safe. Love you, baby."

"Love you, too, Mom."

Three hours later, he was on his way to California.

They spent the first half of the week in San Diego conducting workshops on emergency preparedness in the workplace, and the remainder of that week and the following one in LA schools. Last night they had flown to San Jose and were now setting up in the hotel's conference room for the school training that would begin in two hours. Troy came in as Damian filled a cup with coffee from a table at the back of the room. The hotel had also provided bagels, muffins and fruit.

He took a sip of the hot brew. "Is Delores here yet?" She and Laurie, the other office assistant, alternated taking care of the administrative duties when they traveled. Laurie had done the first half.

Troy was filling his own cup. "Yeah. She stopped at the ladies' room first."

Damian powered up his laptop at the front of the room,

then lowered the projection screen. He fished his flash drive out of the bag and brought up his presentation. After hooking up the projector, he went through the slides to make sure everything was in order.

"Morning, Damian," Delores said.

"Morning, Dee. How was the flight?"

"Not bad. Kyle is picking up the handouts from the business center right now. Do you need anything before I start setting up?"

"No. Thanks." He thoroughly enjoyed his job. Keeping kids safe was a priority for him. Everyone had their roles and performed them to perfection. Troy handled the business side of things—contracts, payments and such—while he and Kyle tag-teamed with the presentation. Damian focused on bullying and communications training, while Kyle handled the security, emergency preparedness and response training.

He was finishing up his coffee when the first participants arrived. Soon the room filled with people talking in small groups and taking advantage of the continental breakfast. Damian glanced down at his watch and caught Kyle's attention. They believed in starting and ending on time. He picked up one lapel microphone and handed Kyle the other one, before clipping the mic to his suit jacket and the battery to his belt. He tested it and then, satisfied, he turned to the crowd.

"If everyone would take a seat, we can get started. We have a lot of material to cover today." He waited for them to find seats and settle in before continuing. "My name is Damian Bradshaw, and this is Kyle Jamison. We're from DKT Safety Consultants and will provide you with the information you need to keep your schools safe from the inside out." He paused. "How many of you are from high schools?" Hands went up. "Middle schools?" A few more hands were raised. "Elementary schools?" Almost half the people in the room raised their hands.

Damian pushed the button for the first slide. "Let's talk about bullying. Thirty-three percent of elementary students report being frequently bullied, and twenty percent of kindergartners. It peaks in middle school, which is often the worst period for victims of bullying." He gave more statistics and launched into a discussion of the seriousness of cyber-bullying.

He scanned the room to let his words sink in. He opened his mouth to speak, and his heart stopped and then started up again. In the middle of the room sat Karen. *His* Karen.

Damian promptly lost his train of thought, and it took everything in him to stand there, when all he wanted to do was rush back to where she sat, sweep her into his arms and kiss her the way he had been fantasizing about for the past month.

Excitement filled his heart. Their eyes connected, and she gave him an icy stare. But he didn't care. All he cared about was that he'd found her.

Chapter 10

The moment Damian opened his mouth to speak, Karen's head snapped up. She'd recognize that sexy drawl anywhere. Thankfully, she was already sitting, because the way her body trembled, she doubted she'd be able to stand. What on earth was he doing here?

Their gazes fused, and his eyes widened in surprise. The corners of his mouth inched up in a brief smile before he continued with his presentation. Not wanting him to know how much he affected her, she met his stare with a frosty one. As soon as he turned away, Karen lowered her head and breathed in deeply in an effort to slow her pounding heart. He wore a dark suit that caressed his tall frame as if it had been made expressly for him. With his height, build and that black-magic voice, he commanded the room with ease. Every woman had her eyes glued to him. She forced down the surge of jealousy that rose within her.

"Are you okay?" Melissa whispered.

No! She nodded quickly and tried to focus on the information and not the timbre of his voice. She tried not to remember how it sounded close to her ear. She glanced down to read the note Melissa slid in front of her.

Did we get lucky or what? Those brothers are fine, fine, FINE! And they'll be coming to the school after the holiday for at least a week to work CLOSELY with us. And isn't it funny that his name is Damian, too? Just like the guy on your cruise. What are the odds?

Yeah, what *were* the odds? Karen reached for the pitcher of water and poured herself a glass. Her hands shook so badly, she barely avoided a spill. Bringing the glass to her lips, she took a hasty sip. She had to see him not only these next two days, but another week after the holiday, too. She managed to get through the morning and felt a sense of relief when he announced the lunch break. Karen had hoped she and Melissa could make a quick getaway, but Melissa had other plans.

"Hold on a minute, Karen. I want to speak to somebody before we leave. I'll be right back."

She groaned inwardly. Searching the room, she spotted Damian and one of his friends she remembered from the cruise talking with a small group of people. She kept one eye on him and the other on Melissa, hoping the woman would hurry up. Her shoulders fell in disappointment when someone else snagged Melissa's attention. Karen glanced quickly to the front to make sure Damian was still there. Panic flared in her gut upon not seeing him. And then behind her, she felt him before she heard him.

"I never thought I'd see you again," he said softly.

She slowly turned to find him staring at her with a blazing desire that sent heat skittering down her spine. "It doesn't matter."

"Yes, it does."

"Why? You obviously found something else to occupy your time." She cut him off as he started to speak. "You don't need to explain. We had a great time, but it was nothing more than a physical attraction. We got caught up in our surroundings and acted on it. It happens. No regrets. So let's leave it at that and be professionals."

His jaw tightened, and his nostrils flared. "Is that what you think?" His tone was hard.

She lifted her chin defiantly, but he didn't give her a chance to answer.

"You're wrong. Give me a chance to explain."

"There's no need. What we shared is over. If you'll excuse me, I need to get some lunch." She stepped around him and rushed over to where Melissa stood talking. "Excuse me. Melissa, we'd better get going. We only have an hour."

Finally, Melissa said her goodbyes. On the way out, Karen noticed Damian watching her with a grim expression. She had never considered how she would respond if she ever saw him again. Part of her wanted to turn cartwheels, but the other part was decidedly wary and reminded her that he stood her up.

During lunch, she toyed with the food on her plate and thought about her encounter with Damian. He seemed upset by her description of their time together as insignificant. Could he possibly have thought of it as more? Should she have given him a chance to explain what happened? No. She was just imagining things. Clearly, she was the only one who considered their time special. The one who, despite her protests, wanted more.

Several times during lunch, she started to mention it to Melissa, but changed her mind. Karen wanted to keep their prior relationship a secret, especially since she and Damian would have to work together. When they returned from lunch, she lingered in the bathroom until it was time for class to start. And she left as soon as he dismissed class.

Karen did the same thing the second day, hoping to avoid another confrontation. With Kyle leading most of the presentation, Damian stood off to the side. He appeared to be listening, but every time she glanced his way, he was staring at her.

During a group activity, he came to her table. "How's everything going? Do you have any questions?" He leaned close to read the answers the group had come up with and brushed his hand across her shoulder. Their eyes met. "Looks very good." With one more pass of his hand, he moved on to the next table.

That simple touch had stimulated every nerve cell in her body, forcing her to remember just how good it had been between them. She didn't know what kind of game he was playing, but she wanted no part of it. At the end of the day, she made up an excuse about not feeling well to Melissa and all but fled the hotel.

The saving grace was that she had the rest of this week and the next before seeing him again. She needed some distance.

Damian unclipped the microphone and placed it on the table. It was Friday evening, and their last conference before the Thanksgiving holiday. He shut down the computer and packed up everything. An image of Karen floated in his mind. A smile curved his lips. He still couldn't believe he'd found her. At first her cold demeanor put him off, but he'd caught her looking his way more than once. And for a split second, he saw it—desire. The same desire that had overtaken them on the cruise that night.

His plan had been to invite her to dinner at the end of the second day, but she lit out of the room as if it were on fire. Since then, there had been back-to-back conferences for the rest of the week. Tomorrow would be his last night in town before heading home, and he didn't intend to leave without seeing her again.

After packing up their equipment, Delores, Kyle, Troy and Damian ended up at a nearby restaurant suggested by the hotel staff. Over dinner, they discussed how the conferences and workshops had gone, as was their practice.

In their opinion, there was always room for improvement, and they strove to give their clients 100 percent. When they got back to the hotel, Delores went up to her room. She had a morning flight home. Troy excused himself to answer a phone call.

"Everything all right, Damian?" Kyle asked. "You're pretty quiet tonight."

"I'm fine. I need a favor."

"What's up?"

Damian pulled a card out of his pocket and handed it to Kyle. "You said you needed more than a first name. I did one better."

Frowning, Kyle took the card and read, "'Karen Morris. San Jose, California.'" He seemed puzzled for a moment, then his eyes widened in recognition. "Is this…? It can't be. How did you…?"

"She was at the conference Monday and Tuesday."

"Damn. I don't believe it." He grinned. "Did you talk to her?"

"For a minute. She's pretty pissed. Wouldn't give me a chance to explain. But I'm not leaving until I talk to her." He gestured toward the card. "I need an address and phone number. Sooner rather than later."

"You sure you want to do this? It sounds like she's not interested in starting up again."

"More sure than I have been about anything in a long time."

Kyle nodded and tapped the card against his finger. "Then I'll find her."

"Thanks. It's been a long week. I think I'm gonna head up and relax."

"I hear you. I'll probably do the same."

They got Troy's attention and motioned that they were going upstairs. He nodded. Damian and Kyle walked over to the bank of elevators and pushed the button.

Kyle laughed and shook his head. "I still can't believe you found your girl."

"Imagine how I felt. I lost my train of thought and was grinning like an idiot. It's a good thing I know that presentation like the back of my hand. Otherwise it would have been pretty embarrassing."

The two men stepped into the elevator when it arrived, and they rode to their floor. "I'll let you know when I have the information," Kyle said before they went into their separate rooms.

"I'm counting on it." Damian closed his door behind him and kicked off his shoes. Stripping, he went into the bathroom and turned on the shower. Twenty minutes later, clean and relaxed, Damian padded across the room to stand in front of the window. Looking out over the city, he vividly recalled Karen's warm smile and infectious laughter. Had she missed him as much as he had missed her? And how would she react when he showed up at her house?

After standing there for who knows how long, he crossed the room and stretched out on the bed. He picked up the remote, turned the television to a sports channel and watched highlights until his eyelids grew heavy. Damian clicked off the TV, turned off the lamp and slid beneath the covers, falling into a restless sleep.

Two hours later, he was wide-awake. He flipped through the television channels and caught the last thirty minutes of an old movie. Still unable to sleep, he pulled on a pair of sweatpants, a Carolina Panthers T-shirt and his tennis shoes. Damian stuck his wallet and room key in his pocket and went downstairs to the bar. He didn't want any alcohol, and coffee would definitely keep him up. In the end, he settled for a cup of decaf. He slowly sipped the steaming liquid and tried to keep his mind from speculating on how long it would take Kyle to find Karen's address. Time was running out. Although he'd be back after the holiday, he couldn't wait that long. He finished his coffee, walked wearily back to his room and fell across the bed.

Damian woke up the next morning fully clothed. His first inclination was to call Kyle, but he resisted the urge. Instead he pulled out his laptop and checked his emails. He deleted the junk mail and then clicked on one from his mother. She wanted to let him know that a woman who had come into her art studio asked whether he had remarried, and suggested that her niece might be perfect. He shook his head and quickly replied: No, thanks.

Done with the emails, he opened his presentation and made a few minor changes based on feedback and questions that were asked over the past two weeks. His cell phone chimed, and he snatched it up. He opened the text from Kyle, and he felt his heart thumping in his chest upon seeing Karen's address and phone number. He sent back a text: I owe u one. Damian saved the file and shut down the computer.

All hopes Karen had of distancing herself from thoughts of Damian were dashed, as Melissa spent the remainder of the week at school gushing about how handsome the trainers were. She brought them up at every turn, putting Karen in a foul mood. When Friday arrived, she packed up and left soon after her students.

She spent a quiet evening reading until her eyes would no longer stay open. Placing the book on her nightstand, she turned off the lamp and scooted down beneath the covers. It seemed as if she had just closed her eyes when the phone rang. She glimpsed over her shoulder and read the blurry numbers on the clock. *It is seven-thirty on a Saturday morning.*

"You have got to be kidding me," she said with a groan, rolling over and blindly reaching for the cordless. "Hello."

"Happy birthday to you, happy birthday to you, happy

birthday, darling daughter, happy birthday to you!" her parents' chipper voices sang, her father's slightly off-key.

She sat up. "Hey, Dad. Hey, Mom. Thanks."

"We wanted to catch you before you started your day," her mother said. "Are you doing anything special?"

"Nope. Just some cleaning."

"That's no fun," her dad said. "You should at least have a special meal."

"I may take myself out to dinner or something. How are you guys?"

"Just fine. Can't wait to see you at Thanksgiving."

"Me, too, Dad." Although her parents lived less than an hour away in Oakland, Karen's schedule often kept her from making frequent visits. "I'll probably drive down Wednesday and stay until Saturday."

"Sounds good, baby. You can get your birthday present when you come."

"Okay. Thanks, Mom. I love you guys."

"Love you, too," they chorused.

Karen disconnected and lay back looking at the ceiling. *No sense in trying to go back to sleep.* Truthfully, she wasn't too excited about her birthday this year. It would be the first year since college that she had celebrated alone. She allowed herself another fifteen minutes for her pity party, then, determined to make the best of the day, got up, showered and dressed in comfortable sweats and a T-shirt.

Over the next hour, many of her family members, including her favorite cousin and grandmother, called with happy birthday wishes. As usual, her grandmother asked if Karen was dating. Her thoughts instantly went to Damian. She asked herself for the hundredth time if she had done the right thing by not hearing him out. She reassured herself she had done the right thing, and that some things were best left in the past. But seeing him again brought back every caress, every kiss and the emotional connection they shared on the cruise.

Somehow, Karen had to find a way to keep from falling for him.

Chapter 11

Karen had just finished cleaning the bathroom when the phone rang again. Every time it rang, she tensed, thinking Andre might be on the other end. He'd called several times wanting to talk, but she always let it go to voice mail. She toyed with changing her number but didn't want to deal with the hassle. Smiling, she answered the phone.

"Hey, girl," she said to Janae.

"Happy birthday!"

"Thanks."

"What are you doing today?"

"Nothing much. I'm cleaning right now."

"Girl, that's no way to celebrate your birthday. You should be living it up."

She laughed. "Melissa was busy and my best buddy ran off, got married and moved to the other side of the state. So who am I supposed to be living it up with?"

"I know. I'm sorry I deserted you," Janae said contritely.

"I guess I could make the drive to my parents', but I'll be seeing them next week."

"Or you could do the next best thing."

"What's that?" Her doorbell rang. "Hang on, Janae. Someone's at my door." Karen walked down the short hallway leading to her front door and peered through the peephole but didn't see anyone. The bell rang again, but she couldn't see the person. Irritated, she snatched the door open. Her mouth dropped.

"The next best thing would be for your best friend to fly up and spend your birthday with you," Janae said, spreading her arms wide.

Karen screamed, and the two women laughed and hugged and cried. "Come in. Oh, my God! I can't believe you're here. I'm so happy to see you. Where's Terrence?" she asked, leading Janae into the living room and offering her a seat on the couch. She started to ask how Janae got in but remembered Janae had the gate code.

"He's at home. He sends birthday greetings."

"How long are you staying?"

"Just until this afternoon."

"I wish you were staying longer."

Janae nodded. "Me, too. Now, you need to change clothes. We're going out."

"Where?"

"Don't worry about it, Ms. Nosy. We're going to celebrate. Just dress casually."

Karen changed into jeans and a navy scoop-neck tee. She slid her feet into black ballet flats, picked up her purse and met Janae in the living room. "I'm ready. Did you rent a car?"

"Something like that," Janae said with a secret smile.

She followed Janae out to the parking area and stood speechless when she saw a limousine. "I don't believe it," she whispered.

Janae grinned. "Terrence thought your day should be special, and I agree."

Karen shook her head. "I'm so glad I dragged you to that concert."

"So am I."

On the way, Janae told Karen about her appointment with the art gallery director.

"How did it go?"

"She said she was excited about my work. She has a

show coming up in December with the theme Great Escapes, and I have some pieces that would fit."

"Oh, my goodness!" Karen screamed. "That is *fantastic*. I knew she would love them. So, how does it feel?"

"Exciting, amazing, overwhelming. I'm scared to death."

"I'm so proud of you, Janae. You know I'm coming. How many pieces is she allowing?"

"Since I'm a new artist—five, with another five available just in case. If they sell well, she'll let me do more for the next series."

"Make sure you email me the dates and times."

"I will. The first showing is sometime around mid-December."

"I'll come down early so we can go shopping. Gotta have you looking good."

"Oh, no," Janae groaned.

Karen laughed. "Hey, you know me. Any excuse to shop. Ooh, Audrey might want to come, too."

"*Great.* I'm telling you now, whatever we don't have in two hours, we're not buying. So you'd better think power-shopping."

"Yeah, yeah, I know."

The driver stopped in front of Burke Williams Day Spa a short while later. "We always said we would come here one day," Karen said.

Janae nodded. "Yes, we did. Let's go get pampered."

The driver opened the back door and assisted them out of the car. "I'll be waiting for you ladies. Enjoy."

They thanked him and entered the spa. The receptionist greeted them, then gave them a locker key and a tour. The spa was decorated in an old-world Moroccan theme with deep, rich earth tones, columns and arches. Karen and Janae changed into thick robes and spa sandals. They relaxed by the fireplace in the lounge, sipping warm tea and nibbling on fresh fruit while waiting for their treatments to begin. They privately enjoyed a massage and facial, then met up in the nail-care room for a manicure and pedicure. Afterward, they changed and sat in the lounge.

"This is the best birthday present ever," Karen said with a satisfied sigh, leaning her head against the back of the sofa. "I'm so relaxed I could fall asleep right here."

"I hear you. I needed that massage. I ordered lunch from a local restaurant, and it should be delivered shortly."

"You thought of everything. Thank you so much for this. I was feeling sorry for myself this morning."

"What's going on?"

"First of all, I thought I'd have to spend my birthday alone. Second, I went to a safety training conference Monday and Tuesday, and you'll never guess who the presenter was."

"Who?"

"Damian."

Janae bolted upright on the couch. "*What?* Damian, as in *Damian* from the cruise?"

"The one and only. I couldn't believe it."

"Did you guys have a chance to talk?"

"Briefly. I told him we should just move on and leave things the way they are."

"And he said?"

"For a minute, I thought he seemed upset, but I'm sure it's just that he's probably not used to women turning him down."

"I don't know, Karen. But I guess it doesn't matter now since he's gone back to wherever he lives."

"His consulting firm is based out of North Carolina, and he'll be back the week after Thanksgiving for at least a week working at the school revamping the safety program and doing assemblies for the staff, parents and kids."

"Wow. I can't believe all this has happened since I saw

you a month ago. I guess you really did need that massage. So what are you going to do?"

"I don't know. Seeing him brought back everything from the cruise, and it's not going to be easy to ignore him when we have to work together. I've got a week to figure out how to deal with him." Her mind warned her that he was another man looking for a good time, but her body didn't care and wanted her to throw caution to the wind. Right now she couldn't tell which part of her had the upper hand.

Karen's cell buzzed. She frowned at the display, not recognizing the number. "Hello."

"Karen, it's Damian."

"Damian?" Her stunned gaze met Janae's amused one.

"Or not," Janae said with a wry chuckle.

Karen skewered her with a look. "What do you want, Damian?"

"I need to talk to you, Karen."

"I don't think—"

"Please, baby. Just give me fifteen minutes."

Why couldn't she resist this man? Sighing heavily, she said, "Fine. Fifteen minutes."

"Thank you. I'll see you in a couple of hours."

She gave him the information he'd need to get into the complex and disconnected. She rested her head on the back of the sofa and groaned. "He's coming over."

"I heard," Janae said. "At least you'll know why he stood you up."

"I guess."

She and Janae ate lunch quickly, and then the limo dropped Karen back at her place before taking Janae to the airport. Karen nervously paced while waiting for Damian to arrive.

Damian parked in an uncovered spot marked for visitors and sat in the car for a good ten minutes. Finally, he got out and walked across the lot. A limo pulled up in front of him, and the back window came down.

"Hello, Damian."

He stared at the familiar-looking woman and searched his brain for a memory. Smiling, he said, "Janae, right? You're Karen's friend from the cruise."

She nodded.

"It's good to see you again."

"Same here." She eyed him for a moment. "You must care about Karen a lot to try to find her."

"I do. I had no intention of leaving town without seeing her," he responded.

She smiled, seemingly satisfied by his answer. "Well, good luck. You're going to need it."

He chuckled softly. "Thanks."

The limo started off, then stopped again. Janae leaned out the window. "Oh, by the way, today is Karen's birthday. Thought you might like to know."

Damian grinned and stared after the limo as it drove off. Too bad he hadn't had that information beforehand.

He walked rapidly to her door, hesitated a beat, took a deep breath and rang the doorbell. His heart started pounding when he heard the rattle of a chain and the door opening. "Hey."

"Hi."

"May I come in?"

She hesitated for what seemed like forever in his mind, then finally stepped back. They stood there for a lengthy minute staring at each other, neither speaking. He took in the sight of her dressed in a pair of jeans and a pullover top. The outfit accentuated every luscious curve that he remembered. He dragged his gaze up to her face, met her hostile glare and questioned whether he had made the right decision in coming.

Karen opened the door wider, then turned and walked

away, leaving him to follow. He closed the door and trailed her as they passed through a cozy living room and ended up in the kitchen. She gestured to a chair at the wooden table. "Have a seat."

He removed his jacket, draped it over the back of the chair and sat. She wrapped her arms around her middle and nervously chewed on her lip. He hated the mistrust he read in her eyes. "How've you been?"

"Okay. You?"

"Miserable as hell without you."

Her eyebrow lifted a fraction. "Um…can I get you something?"

"Yes." Without stopping to question his actions, he reached out, tugged her down onto his lap and kissed her. She resisted for a split second before he heard her soft sigh of surrender. Shifting her until she straddled him, he deepened the kiss as his hands traced a path up her thighs and over the curve of her hips.

"Damian," she whispered against his lips.

The way she called his name made him lose all reason. He threaded his hand through her hair and held her head in place as he kissed her greedily, his tongue thrusting deep. Breaking off the kiss, Damian rested his head against hers. "I'm sorry."

Her eyes snapped open. She lifted her head and met his eyes.

"That wasn't supposed to happen. I—"

"Let me up!" She struggled in his arms, but he held firm. "Let me go. I'm not playing these games with you."

He released a deep sigh. "Will you just stop squirming for a minute and let me finish?"

Realizing her efforts to leave his lap were futile, she stopped and glowered at him.

He shook his head and chuckled softly. "What I was trying to say is that wasn't supposed to happen until we talked. But somehow, I seem to lose control each and every time I'm near you. I need you to know why I missed dinner. That I didn't hook up with some other woman on the cruise."

His confession deflated some of her anger. "You didn't?"

"No. We took a boat to one of the private islands to snorkel and have lunch, or so I thought. However, Kyle and Troy neglected to tell me they made plans for us to stay in the Bahamas and rejoin the cruise at the last port. By the time I found out, I had no way of contacting you or getting back to the ship before it left."

"Oh."

"Believe me, I was *not* happy. As soon as we boarded the ship the next day, I came to your room. But you didn't answer then…or the other three times I knocked. I think the couple across the hall thought I was stalking you." He paused. "So now you know. Why didn't you wait for me like I asked?"

"What are you talking about?"

"I left you a note."

"I never saw the note, Damian. I thought you found someone else."

He stroked her face. "Oh, baby. I'm so sorry. I couldn't even look at another woman after meeting you. We spent two days and one incredible night together. And I don't know about you, but I thought something special was happening between us."

"So did I. Now what?"

"That depends on you. I'd like to pick up where we left off and get to know each other. I want to know what makes you happy and what makes you cry. What your favorite food is, what you like to do when you're not teaching and everything else. What do you think?"

She smiled. "It sounds really good, but how are we going to manage that when, if I'm not mistaken, you live in North Carolina?"

His brow lifted. "We live in the twenty-first century. I'm sure we can figure something out. So what do you say?"

"I don't know, Damian. Even with technology, you're still on the other side of the country."

"True, but I really want to get to know you, and I'll do whatever it takes."

"How about we just go out while you're here and see where things go?"

It wasn't the answer he wanted, but it was a start. "I can work with that." He kissed her, long and slow. The kiss went from sweet and gentle to hot and all-consuming in an instant. He stood, placed her on the table, pulled the sweater over her head and removed her bra. Cupping her breasts in his hands, he reacquainted himself with their feel and taste before running a worshipping hand down her belly to unbutton and unzip her jeans.

"Ease up a little, baby," he told her as he pulled them and her panties off. "So beautiful." She looked sexy, leaning back on her elbows with her legs spread. So sexy, in fact, he had to taste her. Damian reclaimed his chair and hooked her legs over his shoulders. He kissed his way up her inner thighs until his face was buried in her lush sweetness. He pressed the tip of his tongue to her warm, moist center, swirling and teasing and grazing her clitoris. Her hips flew off the table, and she let out a strangled moan. He lifted her hips in his hands and slid his tongue inside her, stroking deeper and faster. Her legs began to quiver uncontrollably, and he didn't stop until she exploded around him, screaming his name.

"Happy birthday, baby." Carefully lowering her legs, he stood and quickly removed his clothes.

* * *

Happy birthday? How did he know it's my birthday? Karen lay on her kitchen table, gasping for air, spasms racking her body. So much for that little speech she'd made about moving on. Something about the way Damian kissed and touched her melted her insides, and she wanted him buried deep inside her. In a matter of seconds he stood before her, gloriously naked and his condom-sheathed shaft fully erect. Her core pulsed in anticipation. "Make love to me, Damian."

"You don't know how much I've wanted to hear those words, sweetheart." He spread her legs wider, stepped between them and eased inside, throwing his head back and growling softly.

He started moving, and it was so blatantly erotic that she was already on the verge of another orgasm. Karen opened herself wider, taking him in deeper. "Don't stop."

"I won't ever stop," he murmured.

Their lovemaking changed from slow and sensual to fast and wild. He thrust deep with rapid strokes, and she arched up to match his rhythm. A torrent of sensations coursed down her nerve endings, and she came in a blinding climax. Damian rode her hard, and moments later, he erupted with a hoarse cry of pleasure.

"Karen. Sweet, sweet Karen," he said, lifting her into his arms and kissing her tenderly. He collapsed onto the chair and held her close, the rapid pace of his heart beating against hers.

She wrapped her arms around his neck and laid her head on his shoulder. How could this one man touch the very essence of her so effortlessly? It was going to take everything within her to keep things strictly physical. She could not fall for him, not when he would be leaving for good after another week. Her eyes drifted closed as their hearts and breathing gradually slowed.

He stood with her in his arms, and a wicked grin covered his mouth. "Let's go take a shower. I really enjoyed that last time. And since it's your birthday, I have a few more *gifts* for you."

Karen laughed and pointed in the direction of her bedroom.

An hour later, Karen walked Damian to the door. They were both smiling. "By the way, how did you know it was my birthday?"

"I saw Janae as I came in, and she told me."

She shook her head and smiled.

"I'll be back at seven to pick you up for your birthday dinner." He kissed her.

"I'll be ready." She gave him a tiny wave and closed the door behind him. She danced back down the hallway to the kitchen and let out a loud, "Yes!" While she rinsed the few dishes in her sink and put them in the dishwasher, she replayed the afternoon in her mind. The man was magical when it came to lovemaking, and she still couldn't believe he had found her. He apologized for going behind her back to get her number and address—he'd enlisted Kyle's help—but told her he didn't want to leave town without seeing her and explaining what had happened. Karen wasn't mad at him. This birthday was turning out to be one of the best ever, she mused.

As soon as she finished in the kitchen, she headed to her closet to find something to wear for their dinner date tonight. The temperatures had dropped by at least ten degrees since last week, and it now felt more like late-fall weather.

After searching for fifteen minutes, she settled on her cream wool pants, chocolate-brown scoop-neck blouse and open-front cream cardigan. Karen sat down on the bed and smiled. She still couldn't get over the fact that Damian had come to her house, or that they had made love again.

Now that things were straightened out between them, she wasn't ready for him to go home tomorrow.

Another thought crossed her mind. They had to work together when he came back. How was she going to keep her hands off him or act as if she didn't know him? They'd need to talk about it tonight.

Chapter 12

Damian arrived at seven with two dozen pink roses in a crystal vase. "Happy birthday, sweetheart."

"Thank you. They're beautiful." First his determination to apologize, and now the flowers. He was making it difficult for her to keep her emotions in check. She directed him to place the vase on a table in the living room, then followed him out to his rental for the drive to the restaurant.

He'd chosen an expensive steak house, and they conversed quietly while dining on course after course of some of the best food Karen had eaten in a long time. As they finished dinner, she broached the subject that had been on her mind all afternoon. "Damian, how are we going to do this when you come back?"

His brow lifted. "Do what?"

"This. Us. We're going to have to work together at the school."

"We're going to do just what we're doing now." He covered her hand with his. "But it's going to be hard to keep my hands to myself," he added with a look that communicated exactly what he meant.

She snatched her hand back. "Damian, I'm serious."

"And I'm not? Karen, I don't intend to hide our relationship. I'll make sure not to compromise you in front of the students, but I need to be able to touch you, hold your hand or kiss you. I don't work for the school, so there's no reason why we can't see each other openly."

He was right, but she still felt a little uncomfortable and told him so.

"Fine," he said with a sigh. "If I'm going to be on lockdown, I need to have at least one little bitty kiss every day, Ms. Morris. So you need to figure out how to make it happen."

She laughed. "Damian Bradshaw, are you pouting?"

He frowned. "Men don't pout."

She shook her head. "Speaking of jobs, how long have you been doing safety training?"

"Only about three years."

"I would have thought it was much longer. You're a natural. What made you choose this line of work?"

A shadow crossed his face. "I wanted to keep kids safe. I used to be a high school chemistry teacher and also coached the boys' varsity basketball team."

"You were a teacher?" she asked with surprise. No wonder he thought teachers were dedicated.

He smiled and nodded. "I had this student, a senior named Torian Williams. He was brilliant—wanted to become a biochemist and was a star point guard on our team. Torian had been offered both academic and athletic scholarships from at least three schools. And he had a great sense of humor." Damian chuckled and shook his head. Then his smile faded. "I noticed him acting strange for a couple of days—not his normal upbeat self—and tried to find out if anything was wrong. I'd heard rumors about him being bullied, but I didn't know how bad things were. I told him I'd be around if he wanted to talk about anything. He made an appointment to come see me after school but never showed."

Karen was almost afraid to ask. "What happened?"

"An hour later, I got a call saying he had committed suicide—hung himself."

She gasped softly. "Oh, Damian. I'm so sorry."

"Kyle was one of the detectives on the case. They found Torian's cell phone, and someone had sent five hundred texts over two days telling Torian that he was worthless and that nobody wanted him, not even his parents."

"The text bombing you talked about at the training?"

"Yes. His mother was a drug user and, unless she needed something, couldn't be bothered with her son. Father was never in the picture. I just wish he had come to talk to me," he said emotionally.

His eyes reflected pain, and she squeezed his hand. "I'm sure Torian knew you cared about him. But why leave teaching? You obviously have a passion for it."

"I wanted to be able to do something on a larger scale. Hopefully we're making a difference."

"Well, you're already making a difference in my life," Karen said, changing the subject and wanting to erase the sadness in his face.

He brought her hand to his lips. "As you have in mine, sweet lady."

The passion in his eyes and seriousness in his voice made her breathing go short. *Oh, Lord. He's going to make me fall in love with him.* "You coached basketball? With your height, I'm surprised you didn't pursue that as a career."

"I tore my ACL as a junior in college. Even though my knee healed and I played my senior year, I didn't want to take a chance of a repeat injury. I still play for recreation and occasionally coach in a community league."

She was finding more and more to like about this man.

"Do you want to get dessert?" Damian asked, holding up the menu.

"No, thanks. But if you want something, feel free."

He tossed the menu on the table and signaled the waiter. "What I want for dessert isn't on the menu. Since you're going to be rationing out kisses when I get back, I have to stock up before I leave tomorrow."

Heat pooled between her legs, and she clamped them together to stem the rush of sensations. He paid the bill and escorted her out of the restaurant. On the drive back to her place, she pondered what else he might stock up on. Whatever he had in store, she was ready, and planned to do a little stocking up herself.

Damian barely let Karen open the door to her condo before he lifted her in his arms. He kissed her with a hunger that bordered on obsession. His feelings for this woman intensified by the minute. Without breaking the kiss, he carried her to the living room and sat on the couch with her in his lap. He fed himself with her kisses, explored the scented column of her neck and caressed her soft breasts.

As much as he wanted to make love to her again, he couldn't. He had an early-morning flight and would miss it for sure if they went anywhere near her bedroom. So he contented himself with just kissing her until it was time for him to leave. Pressing one last kiss to her lips, he leaned his head against hers, closed his eyes and held her against his heart.

"I don't want to leave you, but I have to go," Damian said with a heavy sigh.

Karen lifted her head. "I know."

He trailed a finger down her cheek. "I'm going to miss you."

She smiled. "I'm going to miss you, too. Thank you for making my birthday one of the best I've had."

"My pleasure. I only wish I knew about it sooner so I could have planned something more." He stood and placed her on her feet, then took her hand and walked to the door. "I'll call you when I get home tomorrow."

"Okay. Have a safe trip."

He dipped his head for one more kiss and slipped out the door. Driving back to the hotel, Damian took some time to dissect the riot of emotions swirling around in his gut. This was more than a physical attraction. He tried to pinpoint when it happened, but somehow, it seemed as if the feeling had always been there. Could he have started falling for her that first day on the ship when she smiled at him, or the night he held her in his arms on the dance floor? Was it after the first mind-blowing kiss or the night of explosive passion they shared? From the moment he'd seen her, he felt different. She had touched him on all levels—physically and emotionally. He parked in the hotel lot, cut the engine and leaned his head against the headrest. Now that he had acknowledged his feelings, the next week was going to be pure torture. But when he returned, his mission was clear—get her to fall with him.

"Man, you've been smiling for the past two days," Troy said, lounging in the doorway of Damian's office Monday morning.

"Is something wrong with me smiling?" Damian shifted his gaze from the computer screen as he sat answering emails and, yes, smiling. He and Karen had talked for over two hours last night after he got home. A little while ago, he had sent her a text telling her how much he looked forward to seeing her again and, in explicit detail, what he planned to do when he saw her. Her response had sent a jolt directly to his groin and had him contemplating searching airlines for a flight out tonight.

"Not at all. I'm glad things are working out with Karen. I am curious about something, though." He entered the office, closed the door and sat in a chair across from Damian. "This thing with Karen…are you sure it's not some kind of rebound affair?"

Damian leaned forward and pinned Troy with a glare.

"Hell no! It's been five years. I know Joyce isn't coming back, and it's not like I haven't dated other women. Karen is not a replacement for Joyce. She never could be. They're two very different women. Karen makes me feel like I've been given a new lease on life. She's... I...I don't know." He leaned back and pinched the bridge of his nose.

"Sounds like you might be falling in love with her."

"I don't know. Maybe. But we're only going to be in California another week, so it may come to nothing." He blew out a long breath. "All I know is I have deep feelings for Karen that I've never experienced with any other woman."

"Including Joyce?"

Damian nodded and waited for the guilt to rise. To his surprise, it didn't happen, and he realized his heart was truly ready to love again.

Troy shrugged. "It happens to some people like that." He chuckled. "For others, they have to be dragged into it kicking and screaming."

Damian laughed. "Are you in the kicking-and-screaming category?"

"No. I'll have no problems settling down with the right woman. Now, Kyle, on the other hand..."

They both laughed harder. "Definitely." Kyle loved his bachelor status and often said he didn't plan on settling down anytime soon.

"So, have you told Karen how you feel?" Troy asked when he stopped laughing.

"No. I just figured it out myself."

"Have you told her about Joyce?"

"Not yet, but soon." He was afraid Karen would have the same thoughts Troy had, that she was a substitute for another woman. Damian hoped he'd find the right words by the time he returned to California.

He and Troy talked a few minutes longer before getting back to work. He only had today and tomorrow to get everything ready, because they were closing the office for the holiday. Thinking about the holiday made Damian remember the conversation he'd had with his mother that morning. Since their conversation a few weeks ago, she'd been sending him emails and texts suggesting the "perfect woman." Once again, he reiterated that he wasn't interested in any of her potential candidates and threatened to leave Thanksgiving dinner if one showed up. All of his problems would be solved if he just told her about Karen, but he decided to wait until he was sure their relationship stood on solid ground.

He leaned back in the chair and drummed his fingers on the desk. What would his parents think of Karen? He sat up and rotated the chair toward the computer. He'd have his answer soon enough if things progressed the way he hoped.

Damian worked steadily over the next two days, staying late both nights. As a result, he didn't have a chance to talk to Karen. By the time Wednesday morning rolled around, he missed her more than he would ever have thought. He sat in his favorite chair on the screened-in porch sipping a glass of orange juice. He had purchased the house a year ago as a first step in moving toward the future. Painstakingly, he had boxed up all of Joyce's things and donated them to charity, only keeping a few precious mementos. The move proved to be the right one because there were too many memories in the house they shared, keeping him stuck in a place of grief and misery that he couldn't escape.

His thoughts shifted back to Karen. He wanted to hear her voice. The three-hour time difference made it only seven in California, and he knew she was probably sleeping in and enjoying her vacation. He stared out the wall of windows, finally seeing the sun peeking through the clouds. The temperatures here were at least thirty degrees cooler than in California.

He ran upstairs and grabbed a sweatshirt, then reached for the keys to the shed and left through a side door. Now that he had some free time, Damian figured it would be a good time to prune the tree in his backyard. It took him over two hours to complete the task and clean up. He put away the ladder and saw, locked the shed and went inside for a hot shower. As soon as he got dressed, he called Karen.

"Hey, sweetheart," he said when she answered.

"Hey, Damian. Are you working?"

"No. The office is closed for the rest of the week. What time are you going to your parents'?"

"Actually, I just got here. My cousin Deborah and I are going to hang out before the rest of the family arrives tomorrow. We haven't seen each other in a few months. What about you?"

"Unless my mother calls with a long to-do list—which she usually does—I won't go over until tomorrow."

She laughed. "What about your father?"

"Oh, she has a whole other one for him," he answered with a chuckle. They quieted for a moment. "I'm missing you, girl."

"I miss you, too, and can't wait for you to get back on Sunday. Didn't you promise me something?" she asked seductively.

"Yeah, I did. And if you keep talking like that, I might just hop on a flight tonight."

"Promises, promises."

"So you like to tease. We'll see if you can back it up."

"Oh, I can back it up."

She gave him a play-by-play of what to expect, and Damian's body reacted with lightning speed. "I think we need to get off this phone."

"What?" Karen asked innocently.

He laughed softly and shook his head. "Just wait until I get back. It's gonna be you and me."

"Mmm. I can't wait for that. I'll call you tomorrow."

They said their goodbyes, and Damian stretched out on the bed, trying to bring his body under control. He had been in a state of arousal since they'd exchanged those texts a couple of days ago, and he prayed that the next four would pass quickly.

Karen disconnected and smiled. Something about Damian brought out the naughty girl in her. With all the chemistry they had, it would take a herculean effort to remain professional and cordial around him at the school.

"Karen Morris, who in the world are you talking to on the phone like that?"

She jumped and whirled around. "Deborah! Girl, you almost gave me a heart attack. You can't be sneaking up on people like that." She engulfed Deborah in a hug. "You look good."

"Thanks. I feel like I've been gone forever. It's good to see you, cuz." The two cousins had grown up as close as sisters. Deborah was part of a small dance company and had been traveling for the past several months. "And you didn't answer my question. Were you and Andre talking naughty? I figured he'd be here with you."

Karen frowned. "No!" Deborah flinched. "Sorry. I forgot you've been gone, and we haven't talked in a while. Andre and I broke up a few months ago."

"Oh, sweetie, I'm so sorry. What happened?"

Karen waved her off. "It's fine. He decided that we weren't socially matched." She told Deborah about what happened at his mother's dinner party. Estella Robertson had never made it a secret that Karen didn't measure up to her standards, but Karen never thought she would go so far as to invite another woman to dinner—one whom her son had obviously been dating, handpicked by Estella—and seat her directly across from Andre and Karen. Karen had noticed the coy smiles and intimate gestures throughout the meal and had planned to confront him about all that, but he saved her the trouble. His response: "Well, we have more in common and travel in the same circles."

"Girl, I know he didn't. I would've put my foot up his highfalutin ass." She cocked her head to the side. "Then who were you talking to?"

"His name is Damian Bradshaw. I met him on the cruise when Janae got married last month."

Deborah raised a perfectly sculpted eyebrow. "Really? I've been gone way too long." She hooked her arm in Karen's. "Come on. I need details, and don't leave *anything* out."

Laughing, they cut through her parents' kitchen and out to the backyard as Karen told all. Later, as she settled in for bed, thoughts of Damian filled her mind. Deborah echoed Janae's sentiment that Damian's feelings had to be strong for him to go to such lengths to track Karen down. Though she was beginning to have deep feelings for him as well, she still planned to proceed with caution.

But each and every time she saw him, all her warning systems seemed to take a hike. Snuggling beneath the covers, she sighed. *One day at a time.*

Chapter 13

Karen had enjoyed spending time with her family for Thanksgiving, but she was glad to get back home. Damian had sent her a text letting her know what time his plane would arrive the following evening. Her heart raced at the thought of seeing him again. She loved the way his eyes sparkled when he laughed, loved the way he gave her his full attention when she talked, loved the passion he had for his job. And she loved that she could be herself with him. How had he gotten to her so quickly? It went without saying that the physical aspects of their relationship were off the charts. However, she began to doubt whether things would work out, especially with them living so far apart. Karen couldn't go through another broken heart. Until she was reasonably sure they were on the same page and had a good chance of making it, her feelings would remain a secret.

In anticipation of the extra time she would have to spend on the safety project, she used much of her Sunday doing lesson plans—something she typically did after school—and going over the notes she had taken at the conference. She and Melissa planned to meet tomorrow to outline the suggestions and questions to present to Damian and Kyle when they got together on Tuesday. When she finished, Karen picked up the mail that had accumulated while she was away and went through the stack.

Her heart almost stopped when she saw an envelope

from the school district office. She opened it with shaky fingers and pulled out the sheet of paper. Her heart raced as she read the words. They thanked her for applying, were impressed with her credentials and congratulated her on making the list. "Yes!" Her heart pounded with excitement. Then another thought occurred to her. If she got the job, how would she and Damian make their relationship work? Becoming principal meant staying put for at least two or three years. There was no way she'd turn down this job, and she was sure he wouldn't want to give up his career, either. *Great. One more thing to worry about.*

Late that evening, her cell chimed, indicating a text message. She picked it up and pushed a button.

Damian: Something came up. Won't make it over tonight.

Karen: No prob. C u at school. Everything ok?

Damian: Fine.

She tossed the phone on the bed, and another wave of disappointment washed over her. With nothing left to do, she packed her school tote, showered and went to bed.

The next morning, Nikki met Karen in the office.

"I heard you applied for Priscilla's job."

Karen glanced up from the memo she was reading but didn't respond.

"I don't think you're the right fit for this school, so I threw my name in the hat. Unfortunately for you, I've been teaching longer, which gives me the upper hand. And you know what they always say—it's not what you know, but who you know."

Karen mentally counted to ten. What she wouldn't give to be able to slap that smug smile off Nikki's face. "Is there a point to this conversation, Nikki?"

"I'm just trying to keep you from being disappointed when I get the job," she said nonchalantly.

"I wouldn't be so sure about that. Like you said, it's all about *who* you know." Karen refused to let this crazy woman intimidate her.

A look of uncertainty flashed briefly in Nikki's face before she stiffened her shoulders. "We'll see about that." She snatched the papers from her mailbox and stormed out.

Karen chuckled and went to make copies. This was not the way she wanted to start her week after enduring a sleepless night thinking about Damian's cryptic text.

She managed to make it through the day without encountering Nikki again and thought she was home free until Nikki barged into Melissa's office in the middle of Karen and Melissa's meeting that afternoon.

"May I help you, Nikki?" Melissa asked coolly. "Karen and I are discussing student concerns in our conflict management group."

"I have students in that group and should be included in the meetings."

"As there are no clear and present dangers involved, the information is deemed confidential. But I'll be sure to let you know if something comes up," Melissa added with an icy smile.

Karen glimpsed over her shoulder to see Nikki's tight-lipped glare.

"Karen, I do hope you don't have any more frivolous vacations planned for the rest of the school year," Nikki tossed out bitterly. "I wouldn't want anything to get in the way of you getting that principal position."

Karen met the woman's gaze unflinchingly. "If you're referring to attending the beautiful wedding of my best friend aboard a luxury cruise ship, I don't have anything planned. My students' welfare is very important to me, so I'm rarely absent. However, if something comes up, I have more than enough leave time. I'm sure it won't affect my chances, but thanks for your concern."

Sending Karen and Melissa a scathing look, Nikki turned and stormed out, closing the door with more force than necessary.

Karen and Melissa smiled and shook their heads.

"She does not want to start messing with me," Melissa said, rolling her eyes.

"I just hope this isn't a sign of things to come with her. Let's finish up so I can go home."

They worked for another thirty minutes before calling it a day. Tomorrow morning would be the first meeting with Damian and Kyle, and Karen was anxious to see how things would play out with her and Damian working together. Thoughts of Damian and his text message had stayed in the back of her mind all day. He hadn't sent her any other messages or called. By the end of the evening, she still hadn't heard anything from him, which compounded her worry. She tried to rationalize that his silence might be due to him preparing for the safety overhaul, but in the back of her mind, she had a nagging suspicion that something wasn't right.

Her suspicions were confirmed the moment she saw him the next morning. The spark in his hazel eyes was missing, and his demeanor had changed—still professional, but almost…sad.

"Morning, ladies. Not sure if you remember, but I'm Kyle Jamison, and this is Damian Bradshaw. We have a lot of ground to cover in the next several days, so let's get started. Damian will start walking the perimeter, and I'll take any questions before you have to get to class. Then we'll meet again this afternoon."

"See you this afternoon," Damian said. His eyes held

Karen's for the briefest of moments before he slipped out the door.

Something had happened between their last conversation and now. She had no idea what, but she intended to find out.

Clipboard and pen in hand, Damian went to the school's front entrance gate and noted the types of locks. He had exited the office as quickly as he could. He tried to put on a good face, but she obviously saw right through it. Seeing the hurt and confusion in Karen's eyes only increased his feelings of remorse. How could he explain the occasional bouts of grief that attacked him? This time had been particularly hard because on Sunday he'd actually forgotten that the day marked five years since Joyce's death. It wasn't until Kyle mentioned he would understand if Damian needed him to handle the first few days of the trip that Damian remembered. The anguish of that fateful day rose strong, and overwhelming sadness consumed him. But for the first time, he realized the grief didn't change what he felt for Karen—that the feelings could coexist.

He recalled someone in one of the few grief sessions he attended saying it was possible. However, at the time, he hadn't believed it. He also recalled several men sharing that some of the women they had dated after losing their wives felt they were competing and didn't want the men to mention their past spouses, or had difficulty dealing with the random attacks of grief. And that was the crux of his problem. He worried that Karen would feel the same way, and he had no clue how to go about broaching the conversation. The last thing he wanted was to hurt her.

Damian stopped to jot down notes about possible entry points at the back of the playground, then continued walking. What if she couldn't handle his past and changed her mind about them dating? Laughter and shouting drew him

out of his thoughts. He turned to find children stream-
ing onto the playground. He glanced at his watch. School
would start in ten minutes. He wound his way back to the
office, and a tall, good-looking woman who looked to be
in her midthirties, wearing a wide smile, stopped him.

"Hello," she said, extending her hand. "I'm Nikki Fleming, one of the fourth-grade teachers. Thank you so much
for coming. This place needs an overhaul, and I know
you're just the man to do it."

Damian lifted an eyebrow and extracted his hand when
it seemed that the woman wouldn't let go. "It's nice to
meet you. We'll do everything we can to ensure that your
students and staff have a safe school environment." She
moved closer, and he took a step back.

"If you need any suggestions, just let me know."

"Thank you. I'd better get started. Have a nice day." He
stepped into the office he and Kyle would be using and
closed the door.

Kyle chuckled. "Man, you've been in hibernation for
five years, come out for six weeks and have a dozen women
falling all over you."

Damian shook his head, pulled out a chair and sat. "I'm
not in the mood."

"How you holding up? I know the last couple of days
have been rough."

"Yeah, but not for the reasons you're thinking." He gestured to the stack of folders on the table. "We have a lot to
do. We'll talk later."

Kyle picked up a folder and opened it. "Maybe you
should talk to Karen first. I saw the look on her face."

"Maybe," Damian murmured, picking up another folder.
With the mixed signal he'd given Karen earlier, he wouldn't
blame her if she told him to get lost.

He and Kyle worked steadily over the next three hours
reviewing the school's existing emergency preparedness

plan and flagging any possible gaps, stopping only for lunch before resuming the task. As the end of the day neared, the less his mind focused on the mounds of paperwork in front of him and the more it centered on Karen. Melissa joined the two men shortly before the bell rang. By the time Karen arrived and he took in her wary gaze, Damian wasn't any closer to figuring out how to proceed.

"I know it's been a long day for you ladies, so—" Damian began.

"Very," Karen said, cutting him off and pinning him with a look.

His jaw tightened. "We'll try to keep it to no more than a couple of hours," he finished, hearing the censure in her voice. He understood it and took full blame. They hadn't spoken since Sunday evening, or technically Thanksgiving, since a text didn't count as conversation. Their eyes held, and then she smoothly shifted her gaze to the notepad in front of him. Taking the hint, he and Kyle went through their preliminary findings.

"I noticed that all the gates are locked once school starts and all visitors have to come through the office. Has there ever been any training for the office staff on how to handle someone who is denied entrance?" Kyle asked.

"I don't think so," Melissa answered. "I can go ask the secretary, if you want. She's been here for fifteen years." At his nod, she stood and left the room.

Continuing with his questioning, Kyle turned to Karen. "What about teachers? When did you last have any preparedness training?"

"Aside from last month, I don't know of any and I've been here six years. We have the fire drills, but that's about it."

Melissa returned and relayed that the office staff had never been trained.

Damian added that to his list. "Mrs. Mitchell allotted

Friday's entire staff development day for training. If they haven't been already, I'd like the office staff to be included. Janitors, too. I know we developed lockdown procedures during the training. Has this been disseminated?"

"Yes," Melissa answered. "Karen and I distributed the information the day we came back."

"Good. The staff should be familiar with the procedures by Friday's session."

The group continued for another hour, and Damian was pleasantly surprised by the suggestions Karen made and incorporated them into his notes. He noticed Karen glancing up at the clock and checked his watch. Once Kyle finished speaking, he said, "How about we call it a day? It's almost five. We've made some good progress, and I'm sure you ladies have other things to do this evening." Although he said the words to both women, his gaze never strayed from Karen's.

They agreed to skip tomorrow's morning meeting and just meet in the afternoon. He and Kyle stood when the women did.

"You guys are great," Melissa said, passing them on the way out. "See you tomorrow."

When Karen came around the table, he wanted to say something…anything…but the words stuck in his throat.

"See you later." She slid a folded piece of paper across the table where he stood and walked out.

He was almost afraid to open it, but curiosity got the best of him. Picking it up, he opened it and read: *My house, 7:00p. Whatever it is, we need to work it out—one way or another. K.* For the first time in three days, he allowed himself a small smile.

Later that night, while she was rummaging in the refrigerator for the makings of a chef salad, Karen's thoughts shifted to Damian. She had never been one to let things build up and do nothing, hence her inviting him over to talk tonight. One way or another, the relationship needed to be settled. A thousand and one scenarios of why he was acting so strange crossed her mind, but she pushed them away and concentrated on her dinner.

While eating, she checked her personal email and clicked on one from Deborah. She had flown to New York the day after Thanksgiving with her theater company. Karen laughed at her cousin's rant about the cold and snow. She typed back: Hey, you always said you wanted to be on Broadway, so suck it up, and hit Send. Her phone rang, and her heart rate kicked up. She snatched it up.

"Hey, girl. Sorry I couldn't talk to you last week," Janae said when Karen answered.

She relaxed. "Hey. No problem. How was dinner?"

"It was wonderful. My parents and Terrence's grandparents acted like they'd known each other forever. How was yours?"

"Good, except my grandmother started in on her campaign to marry off all her grandkids again."

Janae laughed, then turned serious. "Have you heard any more from Damian since he came over on your birthday?"

"Are you sitting down?"

"I am now. What happened?"

Karen gave her the details about his first visit, their decision to see each other and his subsequent pulling away. "I don't know what to think. Everything seemed fine when we talked last week, and now…"

"He seemed like such a nice guy. I never pegged him for the wishy-washy type. What are you going to do?"

"I passed him a note asking him to come over tonight so we can try to work it out or…not."

"I hope he does and has a good reason for acting so

strange, especially since it was his idea for you guys to keep seeing each other."

"So do I—" Karen stopped midsentence when the doorbell rang. "I have to go. I think he's here."

"You'd better call and tell me *everything*. Oh, yeah, before I forget, the art show is going to be the weekend before Christmas. Don't forget to call me."

"I won't."

Karen disconnected and went to the front door. After a deep breath, she opened the door. Her heart rate sped up again. "Hey. Come on in." Karen stepped back for him to enter.

He leaned down and brushed a kiss across her lips. The contact was brief, but it seared her nonetheless. "Can I take your jacket?" He took it off and handed it to her. The jacket still held his warmth and smell, and she resisted burying her nose in it. She hung it in the front closet and led him to the living room. "Do you want something to drink or eat?"

"No, thanks."

She sat on the sofa, and he lowered himself beside her. For the longest time, he just sat with his head lowered and said nothing. "Damian, what's going on? Did you change your mind about us?" He lifted his head and Karen held her breath, waiting for his response.

He shook his head. He seemed to struggle with words, and she asked again, "Then what is it?"

Finally, he spoke in a voice so low, she had to lean closer to hear him. "Sunday marked five years since my wife died."

Wife? Karen had no idea what she had expected him to say, but this was not it. She sat in stunned silence for a moment, then covered his hand with hers. "I'm so sorry." She wanted to ask him a million questions, but the agony reflected in his face made her wait until he was ready to talk.

* * *

Since reading her note, Damian had tried to come up with a gentle way to tell her, but in the end, he just said it. The look on her face had gone from guarded to shock in a blink. He brought the hand covering his to his mouth and placed a soft kiss on the back. "I'm sorry for not calling and for sending that text, but I didn't know how to explain." He closed his eyes briefly to gather his thoughts. "It's not as bad or frequent as it used to be, but sometimes the grief comes out of nowhere."

"Tell me about her."

It was his turn to be shocked. The last woman he'd gone out with told him she didn't want to compete with his dead wife and didn't understand why he hadn't gotten over it after all this time. Karen squeezed his hand reassuringly. "Her name was Joyce, and I met her when I was fifteen." Damian told her about taking her under his wing, their growing friendship and subsequent marriage.

"How long were you married?"

"Twenty-one months. I came home from work late one afternoon and found her lying unconscious at the bottom of the stairs. She was just lying there...so still. She'd hit her head and sustained a severe brain injury." He felt his emotions rising and that deep, searing gut pain as if it were happening all over again. "She woke up briefly, then slipped into a coma. I stayed there all day and night waiting for her to wake up—praying, hoping—but she never did. Two days later, she was gone," he finished in an agonizing whisper. Damian didn't realize he was crying until Karen reached up to wipe away his tears.

She wrapped her arms around him and held him tight. "I'm so sorry, baby."

Her words and the way she held him shattered the remaining thread of control he'd held on to for five long years, and he cried in her arms. And she cried with him, whispering that she would be there for him.

Gradually, their tears stopped, but he continued to hold her in the silence. Damian couldn't believe he had broken down like that. He had cried at Joyce's funeral, but not like this. This time it felt as though his soul had been cleansed.

Several minutes passed before Karen asked, "Do you still love her?"

"If you're asking whether I'm still *in* love with her, the answer is no. She'll always hold a place in my heart and I will treasure those memories, but it doesn't diminish or change what I feel for you. I've been ready for some time and was lucky enough to meet a classy and unique woman who I can move forward with into a beautiful new life." He kissed her tenderly and rested his forehead against hers. "Thank you for coming into my life." He drew her closer. Now that he had shared his past, albeit not the way he had planned, he wanted to know about hers. "What about you? Have you ever been married?"

"No, but I came close. One minute we were looking at wedding rings, the next my career choice didn't fit with his high-society family and friends."

Damian leaned away and stared at her disbelievingly. "You're kidding me, right?"

"Nope."

A memory surfaced in his mind. When they were eating lunch in Jamaica, she had tensed and almost seemed reluctant to answer when he asked her about her job. Now he understood why. He listened as she told him about the conversation she'd overheard and about the other woman. He shook his head. "Sweetheart, that man is a fool. I know that's what you were probably thinking at first tonight, but please believe that I would never do that to you. You're very special to me."

"Please don't. We dated for over two years, and his betrayal hurt me."

"I promise I will never cheat on you." Her vulnerability gave him pause because she was always so self-assured. Her ex must have really done a number on her. "Do you still see him?"

"Since I've been back from the cruise, he's been calling and even showed up at the school wanting to get back together."

He went still.

"He's out of his damn mind if he thinks I'm taking him back."

"I'm glad to hear that because he's not getting you back. If he harasses you again, let me know. Kyle knows how to get a restraining order. He used to be a detective."

Karen sat up. "Do you think that's necessary?"

"Probably better than me kicking his butt if I catch him even looking your way."

She chuckled. "I never would have figured you for a brawler."

His shoulder lifted in a careless shrug. "Only when necessary." Damian didn't usually start fights, but he didn't back down from them, either.

They sat awhile longer, and as much as he didn't want to leave, both of them had to get up in the morning. Besides, he was emotionally drained and needed some time to process everything. He removed his arm from around her shoulders and sat up.

"Are you all right?"

"Yeah. I'd better leave. It's getting late, and I know you have to prepare for your kids." He stood and pulled her up. "Walk me to the door." When they got to the door, he turned and wrapped his arms loosely around her waist.

"Are we good now?" Karen asked.

"Since I was the one who kind of messed things up, you tell me."

She angled her head and smiled. "Yeah, we're good. So I guess that means you'll be wanting that daily little bitty kiss."

"You'd better believe it. I'll see you tomorrow." He slipped into his jacket, bent to kiss her and stepped out into the night.

Truth be told, he wanted more than just that little kiss. Sitting across from her today, even with things not straightened out between them, Damian wanted to strip her naked, kiss every spot on her beautiful body, then lay her on the table and make love to her until neither of them could move. He didn't know how long he was going to be able to last without having more than a few minutes each day with her.

An idea came to him, and he smiled. He just had to get through the rest of the week.

Chapter 14

Karen sat in her classroom the next morning finishing her lesson plan. After Damian had left last night, she was too mentally exhausted to do anything except shower and go to bed. She tapped the pen against her chin, still shocked by what he'd shared with her. *A widower at twenty-eight years old.* Never in a million years would she have guessed that as the reason for his behavior. The mess she had been through with Andre didn't hold a candle to what Damian had suffered. She couldn't imagine going through something like that at such a young age. Just thinking about it, she felt tears stinging her eyes.

The fact that he had felt comfortable enough with her to reveal his story in that way floored her. And when he broke down and cried in her arms, she was a goner. At that moment, Karen fell hopelessly in love with him. She still planned to tread lightly because, even though Damian said he was no longer in love with his late wife, he might never be able to give his heart completely to another woman.

Glancing up at the wall clock, she completed the task and made sure she had copies of the graphic organizers the students would need to start their book reports. She found that the sheets—broken down into introduction, body and conclusion—helped the students arrange their thoughts and notes in a logical way and made it easier for writing. The bell rang, and she walked out to meet her students where they lined up.

She passed Damian on the playground. "Morning," she said with a smile. Just the sight of him made her pulse race.

"Good morning."

"Did you sleep well? You look a lot better than yesterday."

A soft smile curved his mouth. "I did, and thank you. I hope you did, too."

"Yes. Very well."

"I'll see you later," he said and sauntered off. She stared after him until he disappeared. When she turned back, Nikki stood across the way with her arms folded, frowning. *This woman better not say anything to me.* Karen kept walking toward the playground.

After a morning filled with journal writing, math, library and music, Karen was more than ready for lunch. She sat with the other fourth- and fifth-grade teachers laughing and discussing the antics of the students. On her way out, Karen ran into Melissa, who was bubbling with excitement about another chance to meet with Damian and Kyle, and even suggested inviting them to dinner. Karen was having a hard enough time keeping her hands off Damian during those after-school meetings and didn't want to spend any more time in a "working relationship" than she had to. Not ready to disclose her personal relationship, she made up an excuse and said her goodbyes.

When school ended, Karen packed up and headed for the office, admittedly a little excited herself.

"So, Karen, you seem to be quite friendly with Mr. Bradshaw," Nikki sneered, stepping into Karen's path. "I wouldn't waste my time if I were you. Someone like him is probably used to being with women who, how shall I say it, have a few more lines on their résumés. Besides, you wouldn't want anyone to think the teachers working here behave in an unprofessional manner, especially one trying to become a principal."

Karen clamped her jaw tight to keep from saying something that might get her into trouble. "I need to get to my meeting." She stepped around her and strode down the hall. Melissa and Damian were already waiting when she arrived. Kyle came in a minute later.

"You okay, Karen?" Melissa asked with concern.

She nodded quickly. "Yes. Let's get started." Damian's expression said he didn't believe her, but she cut him a look that said, *Don't ask.*

They pored over policies, and Karen realized that, with all the technological advances, Melissa had been right. Some of the policies were obsolete. The subject turned to parent involvement.

"We've done this in several districts across the country, and by far, the lowest turnout is always from the parents. I would think they'd be interested in knowing what the school is doing and how they can help ensure their kids' safety." Kyle let out a frustrated sigh. "If either of you have ideas, I'm all for it."

Melissa gestured toward Karen. "This is Karen's area of expertise. I swear she's the only teacher here who gets almost one hundred percent parent participation with conferences, class parties, field trips…everything. When I taught, I'd be lucky if half my parents showed up to anything."

"Don't hate," Karen said.

Chuckling, Kyle said, "By all means, please share."

"I go out of my way to talk to my parents and make them feel they're part of the learning circle. I praise them when their children are doing well and support them when they're not. Once a month, I invite the parents in before school to have coffee or tea and a muffin—something I like to call 'Coffee Chat'—and ask me any questions. It's worked well for the past two years."

"So all we need to do is promise some food, and we'll raise participation," Damian drawled.

"Hey, it works for police officers, so I don't see why it won't work for parents," Kyle said.

They came up with a slogan, designed a flyer and made copies for the teachers to send home tomorrow. They finished stuffing mailboxes and called it a day. Melissa left to pack up, and Kyle excused himself to the bathroom, leaving Damian and Karen alone.

"How about I walk you to your car?" Damian asked.

"I'd like that."

He took her tote out and lifted it into her trunk. After closing it, he folded his arms. "When you came in this afternoon, you looked upset. What happened?"

"It was nothing. Just Nikki getting on my nerves, as usual."

"Nikki?"

She nodded. "She's another teacher here."

"Why would she—"

"She's been a pain in the butt since I've been here, even more so since we've both applied for the principal position."

"You're applying for the principal's job here?"

She nodded. In the back of her mind, she wondered again how they would make their relationship work in the long run if she got the position. She couldn't see either of them giving up their careers.

"That's great. I hope you get it."

He said that now, but what about later? "We'll see. Let's talk about something else."

"Sure," he said with a grin. "Don't you owe me something?"

"What?" Karen asked, trying to hide her smile. He reached out, gently pulled her into his arms and covered her mouth in a scorching kiss. She moaned and slumped against him. Where in the world did a man learn to kiss like this? His kisses stole her reasoning and made her forget her name.

"I don't think one kiss is going to do it for me, baby," he murmured, trailing kisses over the curve of her jaw and neck before claiming her mouth again.

"Damian," she whispered against his lips, "we have to stop."

"I know." He kissed her once more, then dropped his arms. Taking her hand, he opened the car door and closed it after she climbed in. "Buckle up and text me when you get home. I'll call you later."

His voice was strained, and she could see desire burning in his eyes, not to mention the huge bulge at his midsection. "Okay." She started the car and drove out of the lot, peeking in her rearview mirror to see him standing in the same spot.

Damian watched until Karen's car disappeared around the corner…and until his erection went down before going back inside. The weekend couldn't come fast enough. *Two more days.* He could do that. Luckily, his plans were coming together nicely. All he needed now was for Karen to go along with them.

"I don't think kissing falls under your scope of duties," a voice behind him said.

Damian's hand froze on the office doorknob, and he whirled around to see the same teacher who'd tried to make a pass at him the first day step out from the side of the office building. "Excuse me?"

"Don't try to play games, *Mr. Bradshaw*," she sneered. "I know what I just saw." She folded her arms, and a malicious gleam filled her eyes. "I did some research on your company—pretty impressive credentials and not one complaint. It would be a shame for that trend to change." Nikki angled her head thoughtfully. "I wonder what the superintendent would say if he found out the company he hired is doing more than overhauling safety."

"Ms. Fleming, my personal life is none of your concern."

"Is that so? I'm sure Karen's told you about applying for the principal position here. It would be a shame for her to be disqualified for unprofessional behavior."

He clenched his teeth. "I don't do well with threats," he said in a deceptively soft tone. "You might want to remember that." Damian left her standing there and entered the office without another word.

After packing up and walking Melissa out, he and Kyle headed back to the hotel. They parted at their rooms and made plans to meet up in an hour for dinner in the hotel's restaurant. Inside his room, he paced angrily. *The audacity of that woman!* He stopped pacing, remembering what Karen had said about being upset with Nikki and wondering if the woman had made the same threat to Karen. Damian started pacing again, torn over whether he should tell Karen or not.

He had to tell her. He didn't want her to be blindsided by whatever Nikki was planning.

He sat at the desk and checked his email, clicking on one from Troy. Troy had sent the information Damian needed for the surprise weekend getaway he was planning for Karen. He sent back a thank-you message, logged off and left to meet Kyle. Over dinner, they discussed their upcoming schedule and the progress they'd made this week.

"I see your woman wasn't shooting daggers at you today. Did you guys straighten things out?" Kyle asked as they finished their meal.

"Yes." Damian hesitated before adding, "I told her about Joyce."

Kyle froze with his glass at his lips. He slowly lowered it to the table. "Everything?"

All of Me

Damian nodded.

"Including what happened on Sunday?"

Damian nodded.

"What did she say?"

"She asked me to tell her about Joyce." Damian related their conversation. "Then she told me she'd be there for me," he finished. His heart squeezed with the memory of that moment.

"I'm really happy for you, Damian. Karen's a great woman. Are you prepared for a long-distance relationship?"

"I am. Troy is letting me use his time-share in Vegas this weekend. It's killing me being so close to her and acting like we're just friends."

Kyle laughed. "Then you'd better stop looking at her like she's your favorite dessert, because everybody's going to know."

"That bad?"

"Yeah, bro. You got it *bad*." Kyle leaned back in the chair. "If I didn't know better, I'd think you were in love with Karen."

Damian stared into his drink.

"I take it by your silence that I'm right. Don't you think you need a little more time to decide whether you love her? You haven't known her that long."

"The length of time doesn't matter. I know better than anyone else that sometimes today is all you have."

"True dat, my brother." Kyle lifted his glass in a toast.

"Thankfully, we only have a few more days left before hitting the next school."

"Too bad. I'm enjoying myself."

He lifted an eyebrow. "Melissa?"

Kyle nodded slowly. "I like her. She's smart, confident, and on top of that—fine as hell."

Damian shook his head. "Nah, man. Don't even go

there. Mixing business with pleasure is bad news, especially if all you're looking for is a one-night stand. Melissa is a nice woman, and I don't want to see her hurt."

"I'm not going to hurt her. And you don't seem to have a problem mixing the two."

"My situation is different. I knew Karen beforehand, and I'm not looking for a one-nighter. I'm telling you, Troy will kill you if you mess with the business. We've worked hard, and I don't want to see our reputation trashed because you couldn't keep your pants zipped."

"I *said* I'm not going to hurt her," Kyle said through clenched teeth.

Damian sighed. "Look, if you're feeling her, that's great. Just make sure your intentions are honorable. Understood?"

Kyle drained the rest of his drink and stood. "Yeah." He reached into his wallet, withdrew some bills and tossed them on the table. "I'm going up."

Before he could respond, Damian's cell buzzed. "What's up, Troy?" He frowned, and Kyle paused.

"You tell me."

"What does that mean?"

"I got a call from someone at the school district insinuating there is more going on than safety training, specifically some inappropriate sexual behavior with employees."

"What?" Damian roared, drawing stares from nearby diners. He lowered his voice. "That's bullshit and you know it," he said through clenched teeth.

Kyle lowered himself into the chair and mouthed, *What's going on?*

"I'm going to my room, and I'll call you back," Damian said to Troy, and disconnected. Drawing in a deep breath to rein in his anger, he stood and added some bills to the table. "Someone called the school district contracting and HR department and said we're engaging in inappropriate sexual behavior with employees."

Kyle stared.

"I'll explain upstairs." They exited the restaurant and took the elevator back to Damian's room. Once there, he called Troy and put him on the speaker.

"What the hell is going on, Damian? I know you and Kyle aren't messing around—" Troy said before Damian could utter a greeting.

Kyle cut him off. "You know that's not the case, but I am curious about who would say that."

"I know what it's about," Damian said. "There's a teacher at the school who, from what I gather, has it in for Karen. She happened to see me kiss Karen this afternoon when I walked Karen to her car *after school* when all the students were gone. Karen is applying for the principal position, and Nikki threatened to expose us. My guess is that she's going for the same position and will do anything to discredit Karen."

"This is a mess," Troy said. "Are you sure that's all? We've got a great reputation, and I don't want it trashed. Kyle, you aren't messing around, are you?"

Kyle looked at Damian, who answered, "No, he's not. Do you want me to call the district office tomorrow?"

"No. I'll take care of it. I am going to have to explain that you and Karen are dating."

"By all means, please do. There are no rules against us seeing each other. Anything else?"

"No. I'll update you tomorrow."

Damian ended the call and pinched the bridge of his nose. "I can't believe that woman," he muttered.

"Is that the woman who introduced herself to you, sounding like she was offering more than just a hello?" Kyle asked.

He nodded and told Kyle about the confrontation.

"And you were worried about my interest in Melissa."

"Don't start." He shook his head. "I need to call Karen and tell her."

"Good luck with that. I'll see you in the morning."

When Kyle left, Damian removed his shirt and shoes, then sat on the bed. Picking up his cell, he called Karen.

"Hello."

"Hey, baby. I miss you. I wish you were here with me."

"I hear you. It's getting harder and harder to sit in those meetings pretending I don't know you."

"It's not working for me, either. So, what are you going to do with the rest of your night?"

"Right now I'm going to take a long, hot bubble bath. Then I'm going to hop into bed and read for a little while."

He groaned. "I didn't need to know all that." An image of her naked, soap-slicked skin flashed in his mind, and Damian waged a war within himself whether to hang up, jump in his car and drive over.

Karen laughed. "Hey, you asked."

"I guess," he grumbled. "I need to talk to you about something."

"What's going on?" she asked with concern.

"Nikki saw us kissing this afternoon and called your school district's office." He told her about the confrontation between him and Nikki.

"What?" she practically yelled. "We can't do this, Damian. We have to stop seeing each other. I can't jeopardize my career, and you can't, either."

"Calm down, Karen. We aren't doing anything wrong. We can't let this woman intimidate us."

"That's easy for you to say. You're going back to your cushy little office in North Carolina, but I have to work with her. Our reputations are on the line. Don't you know that this could spell disaster for your company? Her little stunt could ruin your business."

"Not when her claims are baseless. I'm not that concerned, because she's lying. Nothing inappropriate is going on, and you know it."

"Well, I am concerned. I can't risk her doing something to ruin my chances of getting that principal position."

"What does that mean, Karen?"

"Maybe we need to back off a bit—starting now," she answered softly.

"Baby, wait—" He heard a soft click in his ear and cursed under his breath.

Needing to expend some energy, and to keep himself from charging over to Karen's apartment, he changed into shorts, a T-shirt and his running shoes and went down to the hotel's gym. He got on the treadmill, started at a slow jog and increased the pace until he was at a full sprint, hoping the exertion would cool the fury racing through his body. He wasn't worried about Nikki. He'd told the woman all she needed to know and had no doubt Troy would take care of the issue.

As he adjusted the incline, his mind went back to Karen. Somehow, in the short time he'd known her, she had woven herself into the very fabric of his being, and he found himself wanting to wake up beside her each morning. Damian stumbled with that realization. He wanted her in his life permanently. He had spent a month thinking he would never see her again, and if Karen thought he was going to back off, he had news for her.

Now that he had her back, he'd be damned if he let a lie tear them apart.

Chapter 15

Damian met Karen at her car the next morning. "What are you doing here so early?" she asked, glancing around the lot to make sure no one saw them. She figured after their conversation last night, he would keep his distance.

"I couldn't wait to get my kiss."

Apparently not. "Damian, we can't—"

He cut her off with a scorching kiss, inhaling the words right off her tongue. "Yes, we can."

She pushed against his chest and backed out of his hold. "I won't jeopardize my job."

"Karen, I keep telling you we aren't doing anything wrong. I'm sure there are several married teachers in this district. When I taught, we even had one couple at the same school." He took her tote from the trunk, gestured toward the office and followed her across the lot.

Inside, after greeting the office staff and checking her mailbox, Karen reached for the tote.

"I got it." He moved it out of her reach.

She looked up at Damian's face. His mouth curved in a sensual smile, and his eyes held a wicked gleam. Her body heated. "Damian…"

"I'm just going to walk you to your classroom, that's all."

She eyed him, not believing him for one second. Shaking her head, Karen led him out the back door. As soon as they entered her classroom and she closed the door,

Damian snaked an arm around her waist and pulled her against his body.

"Damian, we—" She moaned as he slid his tongue between her parted lips—teasing, tantalizing and leaving her breathless. What was it that made him so irresistible?

"School doesn't start for forty-five minutes, and students aren't allowed on campus for another twenty-five," he murmured against her lips, before covering her mouth again.

Karen locked her hands around his neck and pressed closer to him. His hands roamed down her back to her hips. She was quickly losing control and gently pushed against his chest. "I…I need to get some things ready."

Still holding her, he said, "I know. Honey, I would never do anything to risk your job. Please believe that. But I also won't be intimidated by a jealous woman and her lies."

She believed him, but this just added to her growing list of worries, and she was seriously contemplating cutting her losses before getting in any deeper. Damian kissed her again, and the thoughts flew right out of her mind.

"What are you doing this weekend?"

"I don't have anything planned. Why?"

"Would you spend it with me? With everything going on, I think we need to get away for a couple of days."

"I don't know."

"Please, baby," he said, peppering her face with kisses. "Come away with me."

Karen sighed heavily. "Fine."

"Good. I need you to pack a bag for the weekend and be ready to leave Friday at five. The teachers' training ends at three, so that should give you plenty of time. How does that sound?"

"It sounds wonderful. Where are we going?"

"I'd like to surprise you. The only thing I will say is it involves a plane ride."

She smiled. "Okay."

"What are you doing for lunch?"

"I have yard duty."

Damian groaned.

She laughed softly. "How about dinner at my place to-night? Is six-thirty okay?"

"Kyle and I have to do some planning for tomorrow's training later tonight, so it's perfect."

She reached up to wipe the gloss from his lips. "See you later."

"We'll only meet for a short time after school. Do you need me to bring anything tonight? I don't want you to go through too much trouble."

"No. I have everything."

He nodded and left the room.

Karen rounded her desk and slumped down in the chair. "That man is too tempting."

While her computer booted up, Karen made sure she had all the supplies for the art project. She had borrowed one of Janae's ideas for foil art. After gathering everything, she went back to her desk to check emails. She opened one from Human Resources letting her know her interview had been scheduled for the next day. The three o'clock time meant she would miss the last half hour of the training. She'd pack for her weekend tonight, just in case the inter-view ran longer than anticipated. She responded to a par-ent, logged off, then left to meet her students.

The morning seemed to fly by, and the students' foil butterflies turned out well. Karen had them put away the markers and place their pictures on a back counter. She directed them to wash their hands and line up for lunch. Having yard duty left her fifteen minutes to eat a quick bite and make a list of groceries she needed to pick up for dinner. She took a picture of the project and attached it to a text message to Janae. Grabbing her radio, she went out to the playground as the students exited the cafeteria.

"Walk, please," she called out. "Make sure your lunch containers are in the right bucket and not on the ground."

She tightened her jacket around her. Although the sun shone, it did nothing to warm her in the midfifties temperatures. Karen spoke to another teacher on the way to check the bathrooms. For some reason, the kids always left the water on or slid beneath the stalls to lock the doors.

As Karen made her way to the basketball courts after clearing the bathroom, Nikki stepped into her path.

"I had my interview this morning, and they were very impressed. That job is as good as mine. I plan to make a few changes around this place and implement some of my own programs."

Karen seethed. Nikki had been trying to undermine Karen at every turn, and she never understood why. The suggestions implemented had made all their jobs easier. And, with what Damian had shared last night, it was taking some serious restraint not to knock Nikki flat on her butt. "Well, I'll just wait until a formal announcement is made before I offer up any congratulations."

Nikki opened her mouth to say something, and an alarm went off.

This wasn't the same alarm used during fire drills. Then Karen remembered the memo stating there would be a lockdown drill—the first one with the new procedures. Karen's radio beeped, and Melissa's voice came over the line.

"Lockdown with intruder."

The other two teachers joined Karen and Nikki, and they frantically waved the children over while asking what was going on.

Sensing their nervousness and remembering what she'd learned from the workshop, Karen took charge. "Let's calm down and get the children lined up on their class numbers. Bev, can you take Lena's class? Joe, you take Liz's. Follow the lockdown procedures we distributed a couple of weeks ago." They nodded and hurried off. Out of her periphery, she spotted Damian striding urgently toward them, but she turned her attention back to getting the students to safety. "Nikki—"

"Who put you in charge? I don't have to take orders from you. Anyway, it makes more sense for everyone to go inside the cafeteria. It'll be easier to account for the kids." Nikki tried to call the other teachers back.

"I don't have time to argue with you, Nikki," Karen snapped. "Take Mr. Colston's class and get to your room. I'll take Sheila's class." She quickly walked to where the students were lined up. Nikki followed, still arguing about where the students should go.

Damian met them at the line.

"Nikki, did you not read the memo and lockdown procedures Melissa and I brought back from the training?" Karen asked with exasperation.

"Need help?" Damian asked, dividing his gaze between the two women.

"Yes," Nikki answered. "I'm trying to tell her that the best place for the students is in the cafeteria, but she acts like she knows everything."

"In this case, Karen is correct. I'm sure you received the lockdown procedures. The students need to be in the classroom with the doors locked, lights off, blinds closed and windows covered. Have them sit on the floor away from the door and windows," Damian said. "Please escort your students *now*." He left to gather some straggling students.

Nikki stomped off with the two classes, but not before shooting daggers Damian and Karen's way. "Wait until the superintendent hears about this."

Karen and Damian got the children secured in the classroom, and Karen had them read in an effort to keep them calm and quiet. Nikki's threat of going to the superintendent worried Karen, giving her second thoughts about her decision to keep seeing Damian.

"I heard the end of Nikki's threat, and I know you're worried. Don't be. Everything will work out," he whispered.

She stared up at his reassuring gaze and nodded. She wanted to believe everything would work out with their relationship, but between Nikki's threat and the possibility that Karen might get the job, she didn't see how it could ever happen. Deep in her heart, Karen felt she was only a few days away from another heartbreak.

It seemed like forever as they sat waiting. Finally, the all-clear signal sounded, and Kyle's voice came over the speaker.

"I want to congratulate the teachers and staff for a job well done on following the procedures for an intruder lockdown. We'll use some time during the staff development workshop to provide specific feedback and answer any questions. Again, great job."

When Kyle finished, Damian said, "I need to get back to the office. I'll see you after school."

Nodding, she waited until he left to give instructions. The other teacher came to take her students back, and Karen spent the next several minutes answering questions as best she could about the drill. She made sure the students knew how proud she was of how they handled themselves. They were still pretty antsy, so she put in a movie instead of having them do the writing assignment she had originally planned. There were only forty-five minutes left in the school day anyway.

After dismissal, Karen met Damian, Kyle and Melissa in the office. They spent the first part of the meeting discussing what happened. Damian and Kyle reported on what they had observed from staff, as did Melissa.

"I'd like to hear your thoughts, as well," Kyle added, gesturing toward Karen.

"With this being new, I think the teachers handled themselves very well. After being reminded about the newly implemented procedures, everyone took charge and moved the students to safety. Well...except one person, of course."

Damian recounted the confrontation he witnessed.

"Please don't tell me she stood out there arguing. What if this hadn't been a drill? Someone could've gotten hurt," Melissa said with annoyance.

"So I can expect this teacher to be very vocal tomorrow?" Kyle asked.

"Exactly," Melissa answered, sharing a knowing look with Karen.

Kyle cut the meeting short so he and Damian could work on the presentation. With the impromptu drill, they needed to alter some material.

Karen tried to hide her disappointment, knowing her dinner plans were about to be canceled. She went back to her class to retrieve something she'd left and found Damian waiting beside her car when she came out.

"I take it you're going to need a rain check on dinner."

"Yeah. I'm sorry."

"Don't be. You have a job to do."

"I'll make it up to you this weekend."

"I'm looking forward to it. Oh, before I forget, my interview is tomorrow at three, so I have to leave early."

A smile lit his face. "I know you won't need it, but good luck." He leaned down and brushed a kiss across her lips. "I'll call you tonight."

"All right."

He held the door as she got in and stood there until she backed out. As she drove, Karen's thoughts traveled back once again to the latest confrontation with Nikki, her threat to call the superintendent and what would happen if Karen were selected for the position. She couldn't see having a long-distance relationship for two or three years. One of them would have to make a life-altering sacrifice.

She forced the thoughts from her mind, not wanting to think about it. For now, she would concentrate on enjoying her time with him and looking forward to their weekend.

Chapter 16

Karen's heart beat double time in her chest when she opened the door Friday evening to Damian. Excitement filled her with the prospect that they would have the entire weekend together. She'd had a difficult time paying attention during the training earlier that day, especially when they were paired up for one of the tabletop crisis scenarios. Even Melissa had noticed and asked her about it. "Hi. Come on in."

"Hey, baby," Damian said, bending to kiss her cheek. "How did the interview go?"

"It went well. They'll make the decision next week."

"I'm confident you'll get it. Are you ready?"

"Yes. My bag's right here. Let me grab my jacket and purse and we can go."

Turning her way once they were seated in the car, he brushed the back of his hand over her cheek. "I've been waiting all week to have you to myself."

Karen gave him a winning smile and ran her hand up his thigh. "And now that you have me?"

He sucked in a sharp breath and grabbed her hand before it reached its destination. "Baby girl, you're playing with fire."

"I'm not afraid of a little heat. Are you?"

Damian pulled her into an intoxicating kiss. "Just wait until later. I'll show you *heat*." He drove out of the complex toward the airport.

Karen collapsed against the seat and tried to control the rapid pace of her heart. One kiss, and he had her body on fire. When her heart rate finally slowed, she opened her eyes and focused on the passing scenery, trying to guess where they might be going and how long it would take to get there. They ran into traffic but made it to the airport and through security with twenty minutes to spare.

"Las Vegas?" she asked, looking at the sign above the gate.

He nodded. "I really wanted to take you to my home, but we'd end up spending most of our time in airports, so Troy let me use his time-share. It's far enough that we can have some privacy, but close enough to maximize our time."

She had wondered if they were going to North Carolina and wanted to ask if he still lived in the same house he had shared with his wife, but she held on to the question. If and when the time came, she'd find out, although she wasn't sure how she felt about it. Yes, he'd said he was no longer in love with his late wife, but Karen knew that some people who'd lost a spouse had a hard time letting go of their past lives and kept everything from pictures and furniture to clothes—almost like a shrine. Was Damian one of those people? A touch on her arm cut into her thoughts.

"Karen?"

She smiled up at him. "Sorry, just daydreaming. What did you say?"

"I asked if you were okay with going to Vegas."

"Yes. I've never been at this time of year."

The flight was short. After they deplaned, he secured a car and drove to a property just off the Strip. They checked in, and he led her up to a beautiful two-bedroom suite with expensive decor and lavish amenities, including a Jacuzzi large enough for two people.

"Wow. This is amazing," Karen said as she went from room to room. "Have you stayed here before?"

"It's my first time."

"Well, be sure to thank your friend."

"I'll do that. Are you hungry?"

"Starving." It was after eight, and she hadn't eaten since lunch. She glanced around the lush accommodations once more, excited to get their weekend started.

Damian deposited their bags in the bedroom, then handed her the restaurant listing. "What looks good? We can choose something off the list or go to one of the hotels on the Strip."

She scanned the list and handed it back. "Let's hit the Strip."

They headed back down to the car and, after a short drive, ended up at the Cheesecake Factory in Caesar's Palace. Afterward, they strolled hand in hand through the Forum shops. Karen stopped to study the Fountain of the Gods for a minute before continuing. He glanced up at the way the ceiling had been artfully disguised to give the feeling of daylight despite it being past ten in the evening.

"Are you ready to head back?" he asked.

"Yes, but let me find a bathroom first."

"Okay. I'll wait for you by the big fountain."

Damian watched her hips as she disappeared into the crowd. He placed his hands in his pockets and continued on the path toward the Fountain of the Gods. Passing Tiffany, he ducked in on a whim.

"May I help you, sir?" a friendly saleswoman asked, coming toward him.

"Just browsing."

"Let me know if you need anything."

"Thanks. I will." He wandered around the store, peeking in the cases filled with pendants and bracelets. A case of engagement rings caught his attention, specifically an emerald-cut three-stone engagement ring set in platinum that would look amazing on Karen's finger. His heart rate kicked up a notch. Was he really thinking about marriage again?

The saleswoman appeared at his side. "Would you like to see something?"

"Yes, please."

She moved behind the counter and removed the ring he indicated. "This is a great choice. It's just under three carats. I'm sure the lucky lady will love it."

The moment Damian held the ring, he knew with all certainty he wanted to get married again…but only to Karen. He glanced at the tag. The price didn't matter. She was worth every penny, and he'd been investing and saving wisely over the past five years. He searched for an accompanying band and, with the saleswoman's help, settled on a channel-set band with vertical baguette diamonds.

"Do you know the size?"

He studied the woman's hand. "May I see your hand?"

She stared at him questioningly but extended her hand.

He entwined their hands, closed his eyes for a moment, then released her hand. "Your hand is about the same size as hers. What size is your ring finger?"

The woman chuckled. "Ah, seven. Can't say I've ever had a ring measured this way before." She reached into the case. "You're in luck. I have both the engagement ring and band in that size."

Smiling, he reached into his pocket for his wallet and handed her his credit card. A minute later, Damian exited the shop with the ring tucked safely in his pocket. He made it to the fountain just as Karen appeared. He slung an arm around her shoulders, and they started back to the hotel.

The short drive was accomplished in less than ten minutes. He was anxious to have her in his arms, and as soon as he opened the door to the room, he hauled her against his chest and covered her mouth with his. Lifting Karen in his arms, he kicked the door closed and took determined strides toward the bedroom. He laid her in the center of the bed, followed her down and continued to kiss her, absorbing her essence into his very cells. Fighting for control, he broke off the kiss and slid off the bed. He had plans.

"I'll be right back."

Karen lay in the middle of the bed, every molecule in her body tingling. Never had she been with a man who inflamed her body with one touch the way Damian did. The man was the total package—kind, caring, intelligent and handsome—and had a way about him that made the sanest woman lose her mind. And she was in deep.

She heard the sound of water running, and a short time later, he came back to the bed, cradled her in his strong arms and carried her to the bathroom.

Her loud intake of breath pierced the silence. He had lit candles and placed them on the sink and around the edge of the huge tub, casting a warm glow throughout the space. He'd interspersed rose petals between the candles.

"Do you like it?"

"Like it? I *love* it." She tightened her arms around him and kissed him softly. "Thank you. It's beautiful."

Damian let her slide down his body until her feet hit the floor. He undressed them both, then gently lifted her into the tub. "Is the water okay? It's not too hot?"

Sinking down under the water, Karen sighed contentedly. "No. It's perfect."

He climbed in behind her and sat on the step. "Scoot closer."

She did, and he began to massage her shoulders. Her head dropped forward, and she moaned. "That feels so good." He kept up the ministrations until she was limp as a noodle.

He moved down the step and pulled her between his

legs. Picking up the washcloth, he added bath gel and circled the cloth across her shoulders, over her back and around to her breasts. Damian dropped the towel and used his hands to gently knead and stroke her breasts and the sensitive peaks of her nipples. His hands slid beneath the water to her center, where she was already pulsating. Karen brazenly widened her legs to give him full access and arched against his exploring fingers. She groaned in protest when he removed them.

Damian kissed her hair. "Don't worry, sweetheart. I'll give you everything you want." He washed them up, stood and helped her up. "Watch your step." Picking up thick towels, he dried them off and led her to the bedroom. He pulled back the covers.

She climbed in, moved to the center and watched as he put on a condom. She opened her arms, and he fell into them. Karen palmed his face and brought her mouth up to his, trying to communicate what she was feeling.

He tore his mouth away and rested his forehead against hers, breathing harshly and trembling above her. He lifted his head, and their eyes connected. "I love you, Karen."

Her eyes widened in surprise.

He dipped his head and took her mouth in a kiss so achingly tender, tears leaked from the corners of her eyes. "I love you so much."

He guided himself into her, inch by incredible inch, and started a gentle rocking motion, gyrating his hips in slow, insistent circles. Every movement reached deeper and deeper, touching the very core of her soul. "Damian, I love you, too."

His movements stopped and he stared down at her, his hazel eyes blazing with desire. An expression of relief spread over his face. "Thank you." Kissing her, he began thrusting again, whispering tender endearments.

They moved together in a sensual rhythm until she

felt something burst within her. Karen came with a soul-shattering intensity as wave after wave of ecstasy washed over her.

Damian stiffened, arched and cried her name, groaning long and low. His body shook violently and collapsed on top of her briefly before rolling to his side, taking her with him. He brushed back the strands of her hair off her face and kissed her.

She sank into his comforting embrace and closed her eyes, sucking in air as spasms of delight continued to rocket through her body. Her breathing and heart rate gradually returned to normal. She vaguely remembered him pulling the sheet up over them before drifting off to sleep.

When Karen woke up the next morning, she was alone in bed. Her mind immediately went back to the gentle yet passionate way Damian had made love to her last night. She bolted upright. *He said he loved me!* She wasn't sure what shocked her more: the fact that he loved her or her own declaration of love. Although she hadn't intended to tell him so soon, what other response could she have given him, other than the truth? She flopped back against the pillows. Did he really love her, or was it just something he'd blurted out in the throes of passion? Then there was the issue of his wife. Would Karen be a substitute for the one he had lost? The way he behaved and the things he said told her no, but she didn't want to set herself up for the possibility of having her heart broken again.

"You're frowning. That can't be good."

Karen rolled her head in the direction of the door, where Damian stood leaning in the archway wearing jeans, a long-sleeved pullover shirt and black boots. "Good morning."

He pushed off the wall and came toward her. "I thought it was until I saw that expression on your face." Damian took a seat on the side of the bed. "What's going through that beautiful head of yours?"

"Last night… Look, I know people say things when they're caught up in the moment, and—"

"And you think my saying I love you was a result of us being 'caught up in the moment.'"

She nodded.

He cocked his head to the side. "I meant what I said, Karen. Think back to when I said the words."

She remembered him carrying her to the bed, kissing her…and telling her *before* they made love.

He brushed his lips across hers. "Karen, I do love you. I know you may think this is all happening quickly—because it is. But also know that Joyce has been gone for five years now. Let me assure you that you are *not* a substitute for her. I fell in love with your intelligence, your zeal for life and your beauty—inside and out. I love everything about you."

Tears welled in her eyes. "I love you, Damian."

He raised an eyebrow and leaned back. "You sure? Because if memory serves me correctly, you were the one shouting 'I love you' in the throes of passion."

Karen's mouth gaped. *"What?"* She grabbed a pillow and hit him across the head.

"Hey!" he said with mock outrage. "I'm just saying." Laughing, he snatched the pillow from her and pulled her across his lap, covers and all. "You are so good for me."

She rolled her eyes and tried to conceal a smile. "Whatever."

He smacked her playfully on the butt and placed her back on the bed. "I'll let you get dressed so we can get some breakfast." Damian leaned over and kissed her cheek, rose to his feet and walked out.

Still smiling, she threw the covers back and slid off the bed. Her bare feet were silent on the carpeted floor as she padded to the bathroom, stopping to pick out an outfit. Thirty minutes later, dressed for the cool weather in jeans and a sweater, Karen pushed her feet into a pair of low-heeled ankle boots. She got her jacket out of the closet, picked up her purse and went to meet Damian. He stood looking out of the living room window, but he turned at her approach.

His gaze slowly traveled down her body and back up. "Ready, beautiful?"

"Yes." She followed him out and down the hall to the elevator. "Where are we going?"

"No idea. I'm sure we can find a breakfast buffet or something. I figured we'd start in the hotels on the Strip, unless you have someplace specific in mind."

"No. That works."

The elevator arrived, and they rode the fifteen floors down. He helped her into the car, slid in on the other side and drove down Las Vegas Boulevard. He parked in the Bally's parking lot, reasoning that it was a good midpoint. They settled on a breakfast spot and went sightseeing after.

Hours later, Damian played and won a few hands at blackjack. Karen, who had never been lucky, won two hundred and fifty dollars when Damian put ten dollars in a slot machine for her. They ended the evening with the Eiffel Tower Experience at the Paris Hotel. From the glass elevator ride and breathtaking views, to the man holding her protectively against his heart, she couldn't have asked for anything more.

Time seemed to accelerate, and before she knew it, they were back in San Jose and he was pulling into her complex. Both were quiet, lost in thought. He got out, grabbed her bag off the backseat and came around to help her. Their steps were slow; they were seemingly trying to delay the inevitable. She opened her door, and he deposited her bag inside.

"I'm not going to come in."

She nodded in understanding.

Damian bent and breathed a kiss over her lips. "I love you. See you tomorrow." He turned and ambled down the walkway.

She closed and locked the door. Picking up her bag, she shuffled down the hallway to her bedroom. Karen set the bag on a chair and lowered herself on the bed, suddenly feeling very alone. They had two more days before he moved on to another school, and a week before he went back to North Carolina. After this amazing weekend, things had changed between them—their relationship had deepened, and she didn't know how she would handle him being so far away.

Her fears about their relationship magnified. By the time he left for home, she'd have an answer on the principal position. Karen wanted this position, but she wanted Damian, too. Were they on borrowed time? She sighed and stood. For now, her immediate worry was how to keep her feelings hidden when she saw him tomorrow at school. Especially with all the drama Nikki was determined to cause.

Chapter 17

Karen breezed into the school office Monday morning, spoke to the receptionist and made her way to the teachers' lounge area. She stopped short upon seeing Damian, along with Kyle and two other teachers. He stood there pouring a cup of coffee. No matter what he wore, the man looked scrumptious. It was the first time she had seen him casually dressed at school. They had student assemblies this morning, and he mentioned that everyday attire seemed to be less intimidating for the kids. Kyle was similarly dressed in jeans and a pullover shirt.

She went around the corner to check her mailbox and came back to the lounge. Just as Karen entered, Nikki swept past her and latched on to Damian's arm. It took everything within Karen to ignore the infuriating woman.

"Mr. Bradshaw, I'm glad I caught you before school starts," Nikki all but purred. "I wanted to know if you and Mr. Jamison plan to incorporate my suggestions into the new plan."

"We'll review all the staff suggestions," Damian said. "You'll receive a copy of the policies once they're finalized."

Karen seethed inside, but to Damian's credit, he smiled but didn't show any reaction to the obvious flirting.

He turned Karen's way with another smile. "Morning, Ms. Morris. How was your weekend?"

Giving him a dazzling smile in return, she said, "It was wonderful. And yours?"

His smile inched up higher. "It was the best weekend I've had in years," he replied, searing her with his gaze.

Her nipples tightened, and her core pulsed. "Um…that's great. I'll see you later." She turned and fled.

Melissa intercepted Karen on her way out. "Can I talk to you a minute?"

"Sure," she said, trailing Melissa to her office.

Melissa closed the door, placed a hand on her hip and narrowed her eyes. Pointing a finger at Karen, she asked, "What the hell is going on with you and Damian? And don't try to tell me it's nothing. At the training on Friday, I picked up some serious vibes between you two, and that little show a minute ago… Girl, the way he looked at you, I expected your clothes to melt right off you."

Karen dropped into a chair and ran a hand across her forehead. "It's him."

"Him who?" Melissa asked, puzzled.

"Damian…from the cruise."

Melissa slapped a hand over her mouth. "No way," she whispered.

"Yeah. Way. When I saw him the first day of that training, I almost fainted."

"This is so unbelievable."

"Tell me about it."

"So, are you, like, a couple now?"

"For now."

"That is so cool. What do you know about his friend Kyle? He has the smoothest walnut-brown skin and most kissable lips I've ever seen. Those neatly done twists and pierced ears give him that sexy-with-a-dangerous-edge kind of look, don't you think? Ooh, and don't get me started on that body. Did you see how his shirt is clinging to all those muscles?"

Karen laughed and stood. "I don't know anything except they've been friends since they were kids."

"Well, now that you have the inside track, maybe you could hook a sister up."

"You are truly crazy, Melissa. On that note, I'm outta here."

"One more thing. You'd better watch your back. If I picked up on those vibes, Nikki has, too. She's looking for any little thing to make you look bad."

"I know. She's already tried." At Melissa's curious expression, Karen told her about the confrontations between Karen, Damian and Nikki.

"I hope you're not letting that witch interfere in your relationship. Damian is right. There are no rules against what you're doing."

"I know, but we'll see." She'd caught Nikki's gaze as she left the lounge. The woman had sent Karen a look that, if looks could kill, would have had Karen at the nearest mortuary purchasing a burial plot.

That afternoon the secretary called her room and asked Karen to stop by her desk after school. *Hmm. She's never done that before.* She hung up, still curious, and went back to her students. When school ended an hour later, she dismissed her class and went to the secretary's desk.

"Hey, Terri."

"Hi, Karen." Terri handed Karen an envelope. "This came for you from the district office, marked urgent." She glanced over her shoulder, leaned forward and lowered her voice. "One came for Nikki, too. I hope she didn't get the job. She acts like she knows everything and doesn't know squat," Terri added, rolling her eyes. "Are you going to open it?"

"No. I think I'll wait until I get home." She tapped the envelope against her other hand, not sure she wanted to see the contents. "Thanks. I'll see you later."

Damian caught Karen as she made it to the classroom. "Hey. Everything okay? You look upset."

"Just a little nervous." She held up the envelope.

His eyes lit up, and his mouth curved in a wide grin. "Is that what I think it is? Aren't you going to open it?" he asked eagerly. "I know just how we can celebrate."

Karen wished she could muster the same enthusiasm. She'd been working toward an opportunity like this her entire career, but somehow, the moment felt bittersweet.

"Baby girl, you're killing me with the suspense."

She chuckled. It was hard not to get caught up in his excitement. Taking a deep breath, she opened it and removed the sheet of paper. Her heart beat erratically in her chest as she read the words. "I don't believe it," she whispered. "I got it." She shook her head. "I got the job."

Damian whisked Karen off her feet and swung her around. "Yes! I knew it." He stopped, lowered her to the floor and gave her a long, drugging kiss. "Congratulations, sweetheart. I'm so happy for you."

On one hand, she was ecstatic about reaching one of her career goals ahead of the timetable she had set for herself. On the other hand, she didn't know what to do about her and Damian. Surely he would tire of sporadic visits over a long period, and in the back of her mind Karen would always wonder if he'd found another woman to occupy his time with. She couldn't go through that again.

"We can go out to dinner and celebrate. Let's invite Kyle and Melissa..." He trailed off, and his brow knitted. "What's wrong? Aren't you happy?"

"Yes, but..."

"But what? You told me this was part of your dream."

"It is, but...but I didn't think about... It never occurred to me..." She turned away.

He turned her back to face him and placed his hands on her shoulders. "Talk to me, Karen. What's going on?"

She stared up at him, trying to choose her words. "It's just, I never imagined meeting someone like you and now…now this changes things."

His brow lifted. "What things?"

"Us."

"Why would it change things between us?"

"I plan to be in this position at least two years."

"Yeah. And?"

"Come on, Damian. You don't honestly believe this relationship can last two or three years long-distance. I know you've thought about it."

"Why not? We can do it if it's what we both want."

Karen folded her arms. "So what happens if there are weeks or months when we can't see each other?"

"We deal with those times as they come." Damian angled his head. "Karen, what's this about? Are you having second thoughts about us? I thought we already talked about the distance thing."

"No, I don't want to stop seeing you, but I also don't want to wonder if you're seeing someone else when we're not together."

He heaved a deep sigh. "Baby, I love you. I would never cheat on you."

As much as she wanted to believe him, thoughts of Andre's betrayal leaped to the forefront of her mind. Although she loved Damian, she couldn't take that chance again.

"Honey, this is your day. Let's go out and celebrate tonight, and we can talk about it later."

She shook her head and smiled ruefully. "I'm not really in the mood to celebrate right now. I think I just want to go home." She packed up her belongings and rushed out of the room with Damian on her heels.

He didn't say anything as they passed through the office. When she made it to the car, he gently caught her arm. "Karen, wait a minute. Listen to me."

"I worked too hard for this position to give it up." Her voice cracked.

"I'm not asking you to give it up. I would never do that."

"I know that and I love you, but I just don't think this is going to work." She couldn't ask him to give up his career, either. His mouth settled in a grim line, and her heart broke at seeing the pain reflected in his face, knowing she was the cause.

"Karen—"

"It not that I don't trust you, Damian, but I… I don't know. I just…" She opened the back door, tossed in her stuff and closed it. She opened the driver's door and hopped in, but he held on to the door, preventing her from closing it. "I'm sorry."

"Sweetheart, let's talk about this. I know we can come to some kind of compromise that'll work for both of us."

She shook her head and bit her lip to keep from crying. "I'm so sorry," she whispered, pulling the door shut. Karen started the engine, backed up and drove out of the parking lot without looking back. The tears she'd held at bay now came in full force, clouding her vision and echoing the tears in her heart.

What the hell just happened? Damian couldn't believe how quickly things had spun out of control. One minute he was planning to spend the evening with Karen celebrating her promotion, and the next he was starring in the horror film of his life. He stood there confused and replaying the scene in his head. Had she just ended their relationship? He understood her being apprehensive; so was he. He had never been in a long-distance relationship, but he loved Karen, was proud of her and would never ask her to sacrifice her career. And no, he didn't want to give up his career, either. But he figured they'd discuss the situation and come to an agreement. Still stunned and cursing under his

breath, he stomped back to the office. In the small conference room, he braced his hands on the table and tried to
stop the growing ache in his heart.

"You all right?" Kyle asked, entering.

"Karen just received a letter appointing her principal
of this school."

"Hey, that's great! We should celebrate."

"No." He gave Kyle a rundown on what had happened.

Kyle shook his head. "Wow. She ended it just like that?
I'm sorry, man."

"So am I. Let's go."

They said goodbye to the secretary. Damian's disappointment and anger hadn't cooled during the ride back to
the hotel, and probably wouldn't until he talked to Karen.
As soon as he reached his room, he called her, but she
wouldn't pick up. He paced back and forth. *"Dammit!"*
How could she just toss their relationship aside? And why
did she believe the worst? He stopped pacing. The answer came to him immediately—her ex. He knew the only
thing on Karen's mind when she mentioned being worried about him cheating was history repeating itself. It
all boiled down to trust. She had trust issues—contrary
to what she voiced—but they'd just spent an entire weekend together and he'd told her, as well as shown her, that
he loved her. Or so he thought. How could she believe he
would jump into another woman's arms the first time her
back was turned?

His cell rang, and he jabbed the button. "What!" he
barked into the receiver.

"I certainly hope this isn't the usual way you answer
the phone," came the soft reply.

He ran an agitated hand over his face. "Sorry, Mom,"
he mumbled. "Bad day."

"I'll say."

"Did you need something?"

"I haven't talked to you since the holiday, and you seemed distracted when you were here. I wanted to see how you were. Obviously, there's something going on. Well, it's nothing having a good woman can't cure."

"Not today, Mama, okay?" he said quietly. He didn't have the energy to fend off another of her matchmaking schemes.

"Mama? You only call me that when something's wrong. What's going on, Damian?" she asked, concern evident in her voice.

Damian stopped pacing and lowered himself wearily on a love seat. He tried to come up with a plausible excuse, but his mother knew him and could tell just by the sound of his voice if he was lying. He had never been able to fool her, and had stopped trying long ago. He also realized that regardless of the fact that he was a grown man, Gwendolyn Bradshaw would hop on the first plane leaving North Carolina if she thought Damian was in trouble. She had always been protective of him growing up, and even more so in the past five years. "I met a woman, Mom."

"Honey, is this about you feeling guilty? You have nothing—"

"No, that's not it. I'm fine."

"Oh, Damian. Sweetheart, I'm so happy to hear that," she said emotionally. "I've been so worried about you." She paused. "Wait. Then what's the problem?"

"Remember the woman I told you about from the cruise?"

"Yes."

"She lives here in San Jose and happened to be part of the first training session we conducted."

She laughed. "That had to be the shock of a lifetime."

"You can say that again." He gave her the details of what had occurred since then, ending with what had happened earlier.

"I'm sorry, honey," his mother said. Her voice softened. "Karen sounds like a lovely woman. Your father and I can't wait to meet her."

"She's amazing, and I wanted you guys to meet her, but it probably won't happen," he said resignedly.

"Damian Anthony Bradshaw, I've never known you to shy away from going after what you want. So don't you dare start now."

Damian grimaced. He hated when she called him by his full name.

"If you love her as much as you say, go after her."

"I do love her."

"Yes! I can't wait to tell your father. I'm finally going to get some grandchildren," she sang.

He groaned. "I have to go, Mom."

"When are you coming home?"

"We leave Saturday afternoon."

"Okay. Be safe."

"We will." He disconnected and tapped the phone against his knee. His mother was right. All his life, Damian had pursued his goals with the tenacity of a dog after a bone. Some things came easy, others required hard work, but he hadn't failed yet. And he didn't plan to now.

Karen dragged herself out of bed the next morning and stumbled to the bathroom. She had no desire to go to work today, even with her new promotion. At least Damian wouldn't be there. She stared at her reflection in the mirror. Her throat felt raw and her head hurt, but her eyes weren't as puffy as they had been the night before, thanks to the cold compresses she had applied.

He had called as soon as she got home yesterday, but she didn't pick up. Karen had spent the rest of the evening vacillating between hoping he'd call again and wanting to just end things now. She didn't want to invest any more of her heart, only to have it shattered later. North Carolina was a long way from California, and anything could happen during those weeks, or possibly months, when their schedules prevented them from connecting. She moved her head too quickly, intensifying the pounding, and groaned. Emotionally, she was a wreck.

Forcing herself to get moving, she dressed. Her stomach was still in knots, so she skipped breakfast and made the drive to school. Karen wanted to bury herself under the covers and avoid everyone, but that wasn't possible. She had a job to do. At school, she received many congratulations—except Nikki, of course—and started the transition from teacher to principal.

She spent the next two days moving into her new office and saying goodbye to her teary-eyed students. She reminded them that she wasn't leaving the school and would see them on the playground. Karen also invited them to visit her. Although her days were busy, Damian always found his way into her thoughts. Nights were worse. With nothing to occupy her mind, visions of him and the times they spent together plagued her.

Melissa burst into Karen's office Wednesday afternoon. "Is it true?" she asked excitedly. She had been off campus yesterday and most of today.

Karen waved her hand around the office and nodded. "Yep."

"I'm so happy for you!" She grabbed Karen in a tight hug. "Look at you. Principal, a fine man who loves you… Girl, you are on a roll."

A deep pain settled in the middle of Karen's chest at the mention of Damian, but she pasted a smile on her face. "Seems like it. Hopefully, I can follow in Priscilla's footsteps and continue to make this a great school."

"Girl, please. Priscilla is going to be so excited to know you're leading the school. I'm going to call her this afternoon." Melissa posed thoughtfully. "Although I wouldn't be surprised if she already knew."

"You're right about that. We never could keep a secret from her."

Melissa lowered her voice. "Did you know that Nikki went over to the superintendent's office and bad-mouthed you after the drill?"

"I had no idea, but she did threaten to do it that day before stomping off."

Melissa chuckled. "Well, it certainly backfired. After the superintendent saw Damian and Kyle's detailed report, *including* Nikki not following procedures, he told her she lacked the discipline and leadership needed from a school principal and all but tossed her out."

"Are you serious? How do you know all this?"

"His secretary and I have been friends for years, and she called to ask if I knew Nikki. Apparently, Nikki was pretty nasty, demanding to see the superintendent and ignoring protocol." She lowered her voice conspiratorially. "You didn't hear this from me, but that little stunt, along with those lies she told regarding DKT behaving inappropriately, just cost Little Miss High-and-Mighty her job."

Karen could only shake her head.

"Hey," Melissa said. "How about we go out to dinner and celebrate your promotion with the four of us—you, me, Damian and Kyle? I know a great place."

The last thing Karen needed or wanted right now was to see Damian. "Their schedule is pretty hectic for the next few days. And they'll be leaving at the end of the week."

"Oh, please. You can't tell me Damian won't make time to celebrate with his girlfriend."

"Maybe we can do it later. Right now I have a ton of things to do, and so do they."

Melissa opened her mouth to speak, and her cell rang.

She glanced down at the display. "Karen, I have to take this. I'll see you later."

Karen nodded, grateful that she had been spared from sharing the details of their breakup. Melissa's call took longer than expected, and Karen left before Melissa came back. Luckily, Melissa had to deal with a crisis at another school for the rest of the week, so they hadn't been able to discuss the dinner again. It was a short reprieve, Karen knew. At this point, she would take anything she could get.

By the end of the week, not seeing or being with Damian had Karen out of sorts. He hadn't called in three days. But why would he? Getting into her car Friday afternoon, she leaned against the headrest and let out a deep sigh. She missed his kisses and the way he made love to her, but mostly, she just missed sitting and talking with him. She dismissed the thoughts because they only made her feel worse.

Karen started the car and drove home. Once there, she kicked off her shoes, stretched out on the couch and massaged her temples, hoping to ease the tension. *Finally, the week is over.* Her cell rang, and her stomach clenched. She dug it out of her purse, checked the display and connected.

"Hey, Janae."

"Karen? What's wrong? Girl, you sound terrible."

"Gee, thanks."

"Must be all those late nights with Damian," Janae said with a giggle. "How is he?"

"I don't know."

Janae paused. "Ah…did I miss something? Last time I talked to you, didn't you say he told you he loved you?"

"Yes."

"Then what happened?"

"I got the job as principal."

"What?" Janae shrieked. "Oh. My. God. That is *fantastic*! Wait. What does that have to do with Damian?"

"There's no way this relationship is going to survive the distance between us for two or three years."

"What are you talking about? You guys are already doing it."

"Yeah, but as a teacher, I figured it would be easier to move around if I wanted to. Now...I can't pass up this opportunity, and he's not going to want to give up his job."

"Did he ask you to turn it down?"

"Of course not, but I can't ask him to sacrifice his career, either."

"Did he say he wouldn't?"

"No. He said we could talk about a compromise."

"Then what's the problem? From what you told me about that Vegas weekend, I think Damian is fully committed to the relationship. Give him a chance. I'm sure you both can figure something out. Have you talked to him since then?"

"No. He called once when I got home that day, but I let it go to voice mail."

"I really think you should talk to him. Good men don't grow on trees, and I wouldn't be so quick to toss him over. I'm sure there's no shortage of women looking for a man like him. How long is he going to be in town?"

"He leaves tomorrow."

"Promise me you'll talk to him if he calls."

"We'll see."

"Don't let him get on that plane without talking to him. You'll regret it. Promise me, Karen."

"Fine. I promise." So what if her fingers were crossed. "I need to go lie down. My head is killing me."

"All right. Keep me posted."

"I will. Tell Terrence hello."

"Okay."

Karen ended the call and tossed the phone onto the table in front of her. She stretched out on the couch, closed her eyes and massaged her temples again. After about half an hour, she sat up and started toward the bathroom to get something for her head. The doorbell rang. Snatching the front door open, she found Damian standing there. She felt a sense of déjà vu.

"May I come in?" he asked.

She stepped aside. He brushed past her and went to the living room. She closed the door and took a moment to compose herself, then followed him.

He gestured to the space next to him on the couch. "We need to talk."

She chose the chair instead and waited for him to speak.

Damian expelled a deep sigh. "Karen, I don't want to lose what we have. I realize you've been hurt before, but I'm not like him. I'm in this for the long haul and, like I said, would never cheat on you. Didn't you hear anything I said last weekend? You're the only woman I want. I love you. I gave you everything—my love and my trust—all of me, and I hope you feel the same. We can work through this. Trust me."

Yes, she felt it. "I can't give you what you want. We'll be on opposite sides of the country, and I can't expect you to…" Her heart squeezed and she trailed off, not able to finish the statement. "Maybe if we still feel the same way in a few months—"

His eyes pleaded with her. "Baby, you don't mean that."

She wanted to give in, but her heart was at stake, and she couldn't take the chance. Karen stood and wrapped her arms around her middle. Tears misted her eyes. "I can't," she whispered. "Please don't make this any harder."

"So that's it? Didn't you tell me you loved me?" Anger clouded his expression. "I'm not *him*," he gritted out. "Don't punish me for something he did. Don't punish us."

Karen heard the words but couldn't talk around the lump in her throat. She averted her eyes.

He slowly got to his feet, came to stand in front of her and tilted her chin. "My plane leaves tomorrow around one." Damian placed a solemn kiss on her brow. "I know we had something special, and I think it's still there, but I can't force you to change your mind." He gave her a look of patented regret, spun on his heel and walked out of her house, out of her life.

The click of the front door closing seemed to magnify in the space, symbolizing finality. Karen stood rooted to the spot, silent tears coursing down her cheeks, as she tried to convince herself that she had done the right thing.

Chapter 18

Damian slid behind the wheel of the car, leaned his head back and closed his eyes. Knowing she didn't trust him shattered his heart into a million pieces. He reached into his pocket, pulled out the small Tiffany box and opened the lid. The brilliant stones caught fire in the sun and glittered all around him. Every day since purchasing the ring, he had imagined sliding it onto Karen's finger and, later, her walking to meet him at the altar, where they'd pledge their love to each other for all time.

He snapped the lid shut and shoved the box back in his pocket. He started the engine and gripped the steering wheel. Some things weren't meant to be, and it was time he accepted that fact.

He drove back to the hotel for what would be his last night in California. He paced the confines of his room and wondered for the hundredth time how he and Karen had gotten to this point. A week ago, his world shone as bright as those diamonds; now it was as dark as the approaching night.

His cell buzzed. Damian glanced over to the table where he had left it, thinking maybe Karen had changed her mind, but knowing in his heart she hadn't. Walking across the floor, he picked it up and read a text from Kyle asking if he was ready to head downstairs for dinner. Truthfully, he had no appetite, but sent a message back in the affirmative.

Minutes later, Damian opened the door to Kyle. "Hey."

"How did it go with Karen?"

"It didn't."

Kyle blew out a long breath. "I don't know what to say. I thought for sure you two would be able to straighten out your differences. I'm sorry, man."

No sorrier than Damian was. They didn't exchange another word until they were settled in a booth at the back of the restaurant. Both ordered beers.

While perusing the menu, Kyle asked, "What happened?"

He glanced up from the menu. "In a nutshell, she doesn't trust me."

"Why? You haven't had any problems with the distance so far."

"I guess she never gave it much thought until now. All she sees is history repeating itself. Her ex cheated on her. Actually had the woman over to his mother's house at the same time he was dating Karen. It didn't help that I stood her up on the cruise and was still coming to terms with falling in love again. Now that she's committed to this position, she believes I'll get tired of the back-and-forth and start seeing someone else during the times we're apart."

Kyle shook his head with disgust. "Her ex was an ass. But this situation is completely different."

"I explained that, but she still didn't believe me."

The waitress approached with the drinks and took their food order. "Your food should be here shortly," she said with a smile, retrieving the menus and walking away.

"What are you going to do?"

Damian shrugged. "Nothing left to do. I can't force her to be with me."

"No, but you said you loved her. You're going to give her up just like that?" Kyle said, snapping his fingers.

"What do you want me to do, Kyle? I told her we could work out a way for us to be together. I promised her I would never cheat on her. She doesn't trust me, and she won't even try," he gritted out. He propped his elbows on the table and dropped his head in his hands. The ache in his chest intensified, and he struggled to draw in a breath. Lifting his head again, he said, "Look, I don't want to give Karen up, but—" He halted his speech to gain control of his emotions. "I love her, but right now there's nothing I can do about it."

Kyle nodded.

Their food arrived, but Damian couldn't summon an appetite. As a result, he left half of his meal on the plate and was more than ready to go up to his room when Kyle finished. They made plans to check out at ten-thirty and then parted.

Damian showered and packed. He picked up the ring and placed it in his carry-on bag, not wanting to take a chance on its being lost or stolen in his luggage. He only had fifteen hours left—fifteen hours to know whether the woman he loved would come to him.

After spending another restless night, he dragged himself to a sitting position and glanced at the clock—eight-thirty. He checked his cell to see if Karen had texted or called. Frustrated and disappointed, he tossed the covers aside and went to stand in front of the window. The gloomy picture outside matched his mood. *Four and a half hours.* Over the next two hours, he made preparations to leave. At exactly ten-thirty, he surveyed the suite one last time to ensure that he hadn't left anything and tried to accept the fact that she wasn't coming and they were over.

Karen rolled over Saturday morning and groaned. She scooted up against the headboard and pulled the covers tighter to ward off the chill. In less than twenty-four hours her world had collapsed. She'd lost the man she loved. Damian's words kept coming back to her: *"I would never*

cheat on you... I love you... You're the only woman I want."
Every time she closed her eyes, she saw his tortured gaze and began to wonder if she'd made a mistake. In trying to protect her heart, she hadn't considered his.

Deep down inside Karen knew Damian was not the same kind of man as Andre, yet she had treated him like one and the same. Damian had protected her from the first day they met, never ridiculed her job and was happier than she was about her promotion. Her heart hammered fast and furious in her chest. *What have I done?*

The past four days without him had been pure hell. She loved him, and suddenly the thought of not having him in her life was almost too much to bear. Her conversation with Janae popped into her head, along with her friend's warning: *"Good men don't grow on trees, and I wouldn't be so quick to toss him over. I'm sure there's no shortage of women looking for a man like him."*

She'd be damned if she was going to hand over her good man. Karen had to go to him. He had said his plane didn't leave until one. The clock on her nightstand read ten forty-five. She snatched up her cell and scrolled through the contacts until she came to the number of the hotel where he was staying.

"Yes, can you please connect me to Damian Bradshaw's room?" Karen said as soon as the hotel clerk answered.

"One moment please."

"Come on, come on," she mumbled under her breath.

The clerk came back on the line. "I'm sorry, but Mr. Bradshaw just checked out."

No, no, no. "Thank you." She hung up, threw off the covers and dashed to the bathroom.

She brushed her teeth, washed her face and dressed in ten minutes. Grabbing the brush, she slicked her hair back and slid on a headband. After sticking her feet in a pair of running shoes and grabbing her jacket, purse and keys, she sprinted out to her car. Karen stuck the key in, gunned the engine and sped out of the complex toward the airport. She didn't have a clue what she would say, but she couldn't let him leave without at least telling him she loved him. On the drive, she realized she didn't know the airline or terminal. Engaging her Bluetooth, she called Janae.

"Hey, Janae. I don't have time to explain, but I need you to go online and tell me which airline has a flight out of San Jose to Charlotte, North Carolina, today leaving around one."

"Is this about Damian?"

She choked back a sob. "Yes. I messed up, and he's leaving."

"Okay. Hang on." Janae paused. "There's a Delta flight leaving at one-twenty."

"Thank you," Karen breathed.

"Now go get your man."

"I owe you."

"That's what friends are for. Later."

Fifteen minutes later, Karen parked in the daily lot outside Terminal A and ran across the street. She searched frantically for several minutes at the counters and around the lower level. Her heart sank upon not seeing him. And there was no way to get through security without a ticket.

Pacing and rubbing her hand across her forehead, she muttered over and over, "Think, Karen, think." She stopped and made a beeline for the counter. Maybe she could have him paged. Halfway there, she saw him and Kyle walk through the far doors, and her heart lurched.

"Damian! Damian!" she screamed, running toward him and not caring about the people staring at her.

He whirled around, and their eyes locked. His face was unreadable, and her steps slowed until she was standing in front of him.

"Hey, Karen," Kyle said. "I'll wait for you over by the

café, Damian." He gave Karen an encouraging smile and
sauntered off.

She and Damian stood in strained silence. "Hi," she
finally said.

"Hey."

She wrung her hands, not knowing how to begin.

"Why are you here?"

"I owe you an apology, Damian. I should've talked to
you, tried to work it out, and I should have believed that
you're a man of your word."

He cocked his head to the side. "And you do now?"

"Yes. I'm so sorry."

Damian paused, then nodded. "Apology accepted." He
turned to walk away.

"Wait," she called anxiously, latching on to his arm.

He tensed.

"Please, wait."

He slowly faced her.

She dropped her hand. He didn't plan to make things
easy for her, and she guessed she deserved it. "I love you,
Damian, more than anything. And I do trust you."

He placed his hands on her shoulders. "Is that all?"

"No. I'm ready."

He moved his hands down to her waist and pulled her
closer, a smile tugging at his lips. "Ready for what?"

She took a deep breath. "To give you what you want."

"And what's that?"

"Everything. My love, my trust...all of me. I know it's
not going to be easy, but I need you in my life."

He hauled her against the solid wall of his chest and
wrapped her in a crushing hug.

"I love you, Karen. I love you, baby. I didn't think you'd
come. We'll do whatever it takes to make this work."

Tears of relief sprang from her eyes.

He leaned back, and she saw the sheen of tears in his

eyes. Keeping one hand around her waist, he used the other one to tip her chin up. "Promise me you won't ever push me away again."

"I won't," she cried.

Damian lowered his head and covered her mouth in a tender but heated kiss. He peppered her face with kisses before claiming her mouth again and telling her how glad he was that she came.

Karen held him tight, not wanting him to leave.

"I don't want to leave you," he whispered against her ear.

"I wish you didn't have to go."

"Come home with me."

She jerked back. "Come home with you? What? When?"

"Now."

"Now?" She searched his face. "Are you serious?"

"Very. I want you to meet my parents."

She glanced down at the oversize sweatshirt and old pair of jeans she had hastily thrown on and shook her head vehemently. "I can't go with you. I don't have a ticket, clothes…"

"I'll get you a ticket, and we can shop for everything you need."

"But—"

He put his finger on her lips. "Please. I want them to meet you."

"I don't know. This is crazy." But at the same time, she didn't want to be away from him. Then there was the curiosity about his house. "I have to go to work on Monday."

"Give me twenty-four hours, baby girl. That's all I'm asking." He unleashed that captivating smile on her, and she caved.

"Okay." The words were barely off her tongue when he grabbed her by the hand and dragged her over to the line to purchase a ticket. Everything happened so fast, her head spun.

"You okay?"

"It's just that everything is going so fast. I'm trying to catch up, that's all."

They reached the counter, and he pulled out his travel documents. Luckily, there were seats available. She handed over her driver's license, and a minute later she had a ticket. She would return on a 5:00 p.m. flight tomorrow. Smiling, they went through security and proceeded to the gate. When the time came to board, Karen was surprised to find herself seated in first class. She hadn't bothered to look at the ticket, but guessed with Damian's and Kyle's height, they definitely wouldn't be comfortable in coach.

Damian reached down for her hand. "You good, baby?"

She smiled and snuggled closer. "Better than good."

Two planes, a taxi and over seven hours later, Damian opened the door to his house and moved aside so she could enter. Given the late hour, she could only tell that the house was brick and had a nice porch.

He set his bags down in the foyer. Bending, Damian swept her up in his arms and strode purposely from the room and upstairs. "It's late. Let's go get comfortable. You can see the house tomorrow. We'll put your clothes in the washer tonight and go shopping in the morning."

"I don't have anything to sleep in." She had bought a toothbrush, toothpaste, comb, brush and deodorant in one of the airport shops.

"You won't need anything tonight. I'll keep you warm," he said, pressing a wall switch and entering his bedroom. He placed her on her feet.

She laughed. He was right. "Very nice," she said, turning in a slow circle. Dark, heavy furniture dominated the space with a huge bed as the focal point, decorated in soft gray hues.

"Come on. You can get your shower first."

She followed him into the bathroom done in gray and black marble.

He turned on the water and placed towels on the counter. "I'll bring you a shirt." He left and returned with a black T-shirt. "Enjoy."

"Thanks." She closed the door behind him, undressed and stepped into the heated space. She washed up, careful not to wet her hair, and contemplated her whirlwind of a day. At best, she figured they'd patch things up with a promise to visit in a couple of weeks. She never dreamed she would hop on a plane to go home with him or meet his parents. He promised to show her the house tomorrow, and Karen couldn't help being apprehensive. So far, nothing in his bedroom indicated the presence of his late wife, but would that hold for the rest of the house?

Chapter 19

While Karen showered, Damian went downstairs to retrieve his bags and turn off the lights. He still couldn't believe she had come. His heart had filled to near bursting when he heard her calling out to him, and it was all he could do to stand there. But he needed to hear her say the words, to tell him she trusted him and believed in him—in them. Back in his bedroom, he placed his suitcase in a corner and his carry-on bag on a chair. Unzipping an inside pocket, he took out the jeweler's box, clutched it in his palm and offered up a prayer of thanks. With any luck, the ring would end up exactly where it should be.

He walked down the hallway to a second bathroom and showered. When he returned, Karen was just coming out of the bathroom. Like any man, he got a thrill from seeing her in his shirt. He stood nearly a foot taller than her, so the shirt went almost to her knees.

She held up her clothes. "Can I put these in the washer?"

"Follow me." He led her back downstairs to the laundry room and waited while she started the washer, then carried her back upstairs.

He pulled the covers back on the bed and made a mental note to thank his housekeeper for changing the sheets. Damian placed Karen on the bed, climbed in and pulled her into his arms. He groaned with contentment.

"I'm so glad you came," he said, brushing a kiss across her lips. "So glad."

"Me, too."

He kissed her again and set about showing her just how happy he was.

Damian woke up the following morning, braced on his elbow and watched Karen sleep. Twenty-four hours ago, he thought he'd have to live without this remarkable woman. He wanted her by his side for always and didn't know how he was going to let her go this afternoon.

"Karen." He nuzzled her neck. "Wake up, sleepyhead. Time to get moving."

Her eyes fluttered, then opened slowly. "Mmm, morning. What time is it?"

"Morning. Just after eight. We have a lot to pack in before you leave."

She buried her face in his chest. "I wish I didn't have to go."

"So do I, baby. We have a couple of workshops scheduled this week. Otherwise I'd go back with you. The earliest I can fly down is Friday."

Karen groaned. "I'm going to LA on Friday. Janae is having her first art showing that night."

"Can you bring a guest?"

She lifted her head, and a smile lit her face. "You'll come to LA with me?"

"Sweetheart, I'll follow you anywhere. Do you still want to go shopping? Your clothes are on the bench at the foot of the bed."

"Yes. I can't meet your parents wearing a sweatshirt and old jeans."

He laughed. "You look beautiful in anything, and my parents won't care. If it'll make you more comfortable, I'll dress the same way."

"It doesn't. So let's go. You don't introduce somebody to your parents dressed like a hobo off the streets." She flipped the covers back, hopped up and grabbed her clothes off the bench. Still muttering under her breath, she cut him a look, went into the bathroom and slammed the door.

Damian fell back against the pillows and howled with laughter. When she was done dressing, they toured the house. He started with the two other upstairs bedrooms before heading down to the lower level and stopping first at his home office. He watched Karen wander around the room, then over to his desk. He held his breath, waiting for her response, when she picked up the small picture of Joyce. He had a few more photos, the banner Joyce had made for him when he got his first teaching job and the locket he'd given her when she graduated from college, all in a box kept in the hall closet. Everything else was gone.

"She's beautiful," Karen said.

"She was." He waited for her to say something else, but she replaced the picture and followed him out.

Damian escorted Karen through a formal living room with expensive but comfortable-looking furniture, a spacious gourmet kitchen and a large family room with leather furniture and a huge flat-screen television mounted on the wall. He went left and into a beautiful screened-in porch that looked lived-in.

"This is lovely. You must spend a lot of time here. I know I would." There were three walls of windows, two loungers and a small table between matching oversize chairs in front of a fireplace. It was the ultimate relaxation space.

"I do. It's the biggest reason I purchased the house."

Scanning the area, she wondered if he had spent hours out here with his late wife.

As if he had interpreted her thoughts, he said, "I bought it a year ago." He wrapped his arms around her. "You're the first woman who's been here."

She glanced over her shoulder at him, then turned back toward the windows. "Was it hard to leave your old house?"

"At first, yes. After a while, I felt like I was starting to suffocate and I couldn't pull myself out of it. I went to counseling for a while and realized I had been trapped in the same cycle of grief for four years. Moving helped tremendously. I even went out on a few dates." He turned her in his arms. "But no one made me want to try to love again until you. Don't ever think you're a substitute for another woman. You could never be one." He kissed her tenderly. "I love you, Karen."

Coming home with him had been the right decision. She needed to hear those words from him—needed reassurance of her place in his life. "I love you, too."

"Let's go get some breakfast."

Damian drove them to a local restaurant, grateful that they'd hurdled that issue. While eating, they talked, laughed and began the discussion of their long-distance relationship commitment. An hour later, he pulled into the mall parking lot. It didn't take her long to find what she needed. Karen added a tote bag and carried everything to the register. He overrode her protests to pay and placed his credit card on the counter.

"This impromptu trip was my idea, so it's only fair that I cover any expenses," he reasoned. They engaged in a stare-down until she finally relented.

"Fine, you win."

He gave her a quick kiss. "Thank you." He signed the receipt, picked up the bags and escorted her back out. "We'll go home so you can change, then head over to my parents'."

He drove home and carried her bags inside. Upstairs in his bedroom, he watched her pull out a curling iron, makeup and a host of other things. He shook his head. "Honey, we're not going to dinner at the White House, just over to my parents'."

"I know, but I want to look nice."

"What you're wearing is fine."

She placed her hands on her hips. "Damian Bradshaw, I am *not* wearing—"

He held up his hands in surrender. "Okay, okay. I'll wait for you on the porch."

"I won't be long." She gathered up her haul and went into the bathroom.

Damian's heart raced with excitement. He never thought he would risk his heart again—the pain of losing had been too much. Since meeting Karen, he realized the pain of not having her in his life outweighed everything else. He couldn't wait to introduce her to his parents.

Karen surveyed herself one last time. She wanted to look especially nice for his parents. Would they like her? Or would they compare her to his first wife?

When she toured the rest of the house, she saw that he kept only one small picture of Joyce in his office—nothing like the shrine Karen had envisioned. But Joyce was a beautiful young woman, and Karen couldn't help wondering how his parents would feel about him marrying again. She took a deep breath and tried to still the butterflies fluttering in her belly. She placed her stuff in the tote bag, turned off the light and made her way to the porch.

Damian stood facing the window with his feet braced apart and his arms folded across his chest, seemingly deep in thought. She crossed the floor and touched his arm. "You okay?"

He wrapped an arm around her shoulders and dropped a kiss on her hair. "I'm good. You look beautiful."

"Thanks. I'm ready, if you are."

On the way over, she wondered again how they would make the relationship work. "How are we going to do this, Damian?"

Damian's gaze slid to hers briefly, then back to the road. "Do what?"

"This. Us."

They came to a red light, and Damian reached over and covered her hand. "Baby, like I told you over breakfast, we *will* figure out what'll work best for both of us. Relax."

"Okay." She resumed watching the passing scenery. A few minutes later, Damian pulled into the driveway of a one-story brick ranch-style house on the corner with a circular driveway. She saw a smaller attached structure and asked about it.

"My mom has an art studio. It's connected to the house through a breezeway."

"An art studio? That sounds so cool."

"Yep."

"What type of art does she do?"

"Sculptures. I'm sure she'll give you a tour if you ask."

Just then, a tall, slender woman with the same golden-colored skin as Damian opened the front door. "Did your parents know you were bringing a guest?"

"Nah. I wanted to surprise them."

"I am so going to kill you, Damian. You're gonna give them a heart attack."

Damian laughed, hopped out and came around to her side.

He helped her out of the car and she whispered, "You'd better be right." He kissed her, and she saw his mother's eyes widen. Karen groaned and let him lead her up the walkway.

"Hey, Mom," he said, bending to kiss her cheek.

"Hi, sweetheart. Welcome back. And who is this lovely young woman?" she asked with a warm smile.

"Mom, I want you to meet Karen Morris. Karen, this is my mother, Gwendolyn Bradshaw."

"It's very nice to meet you, Mrs. Bradshaw," Karen said, extending her hand.

"I'm so happy to finally meet you, Karen," she said, ignoring Karen's hand and pulling her into a warm embrace. "Please come in. Louis is going to be so tickled to meet you."

Karen followed her through the foyer and large living room to an even larger family room, where a walnut-colored older version of Damian sat watching a basketball game.

"Louis, this is Damian's girl, Karen," Mrs. Bradshaw said.

He rose to his feet swiftly and engulfed her in a bear hug. "Welcome, Karen. It's nice to meet you. Make yourself comfortable."

"Thank you. It's nice to meet you, too."

He turned to Damian and pulled him into a rough hug. "Welcome back, son." His parents traded secret smiles.

When they were comfortably seated, Mrs. Bradshaw said, "Karen, tell me about yourself."

"I teach fourth grade."

Damian cleared his throat, and she smiled at him. "Actually, I've just been appointed principal."

"Congratulations. That's wonderful."

They spent another hour with his parents—his mother insisted on fixing an elaborate lunch—getting to know one another, and leaving no doubt in Karen's mind that she wouldn't be standing in the shadow of another woman. When the time came for Karen to leave, Damian's parents walked them out and again expressed their happiness. She waved at them until they were out of her sight. On the drive to the airport, she and Damian spoke very little, both reluctant to part. He parked in the lot and walked her inside.

He kissed her deeply. "I love you so much."

"I love you, too." She turned and started to walk away,

but Damian held on to her hand. "I can't leave if you're holding my hand. You have to let go."

"I can't let you go."

She chuckled. "What do you mean you can't let me go? I have a plane to catch and work to go to in the morning."

"I can't let you go—not without you agreeing to be my wife."

"Wait!" She gasped and stared at him in shock. "What did you…? Your *what*?"

Damian dropped to one knee in front of her. "Karen, I never thought I'd be able to give my heart again, but then you came along. Your presence calms me, your touch comforts me and your love reminds me what's most important each day. When I look at you, I know the love we share will continue to grow. You mean everything to me. Marry me. Let me give you all of me from this day forth."

Tears began to fall before he could finish and ask the question. "Yes, I'll marry you." She lowered to her knees to match him. "And I want to give you all of me."

He reached into his bag and pulled out a small box from Tiffany. Her eyes widened like saucers when she saw the ring nestled inside. He slid it on her finger. It fit perfectly. "Oh. My. God. It's *amazing*," she whispered through her tears. She launched herself at him, knocking him to the floor. "I love you, Damian."

Laughing, he said, "I love you, too."

They lay on the floor kissing until he said, "If you don't let me up off this hard floor, you're going to miss your plane."

She groaned and buried her head in his chest. Someone tapped her on the shoulder, and she looked up to see a smiling Kyle. Karen sprang up, hearing the clapping and whistling.

"I can't wait to show Troy this video," Kyle said with

a laugh, holding up his cell. "That was some proposal. Congratulations."

Her mouth fell open. "What? How did you…?" She narrowed her gaze at Damian. "Did you do this?"

He smiled and shrugged. "I wanted proof, just in case you changed your mind."

She shook her head. "I don't know what I'm going to do with you, Damian Bradshaw."

He laughed. "Hey, you're stuck with me now, for better or worse."

She glanced down at the ring on her finger, then back up at him. "Yeah, I am, huh?"

He kissed her once more and held her tightly against him. "You'd better go. Call me when you get home. I love you."

Holding him tight, she whispered, "I will. I love you, too." Karen released him and then walked away while she still could.

The trip home seemed much longer, but the knowledge that she would see Damian the following weekend and the exquisite ring on her finger made it bearable. She giggled to herself. *Grandma can scratch me off her matchmaking list.* She couldn't wait to see her parents' faces when she told them.

She and Damian still had a lot to work out, but Karen felt confident about their future together. She stared, once again, at the ring on her finger and knew she would love him forever.

Epilogue

One year later

"So, how does it feel to know in less than thirty minutes you'll be a married woman?" Janae asked, coming into the room where Karen waited for the wedding to begin.

"I'm so excited, I can barely stand it."

"This dress is spectacular."

Karen walked over to the mirror and ran her hand down the front of the strapless beaded gown with a sweetheart neckline, lace-up back and trumpet skirt. "I fell in love with this dress the moment I saw it."

"I think Damian's going to fall in love with it, as well." Janae wiped a hand across her forehead.

Noticing the slight frown on Janae's face, Karen turned from the mirror. "Are you okay?"

Janae waved her off. "I'm fine. Just a little light-headed and queasy."

"Janae? What are you telling me?" Janae paused, and Karen called her name again.

Finally, she smiled faintly and said, "You're going to be a godmother."

Karen's eyes filled with tears, and she hugged her friend. "I am so excited for you and Terrence."

"Thank you. But today is all about you. Don't go ruining your makeup with all this crying," she said, laughing. "No tears allowed."

Karen pulled a tissue from the box sitting on the counter, handed Janae one and turned back to the mirror. She dabbed at the corners of her eyes, being careful not to smudge the mascara and liner.

"So, are you ready to admit I was right?" Janae asked.

"What are you talking about?"

"Remember Terrence's concert on the cruise? I reminded you about what happened the first time we went to his concert—one of us ended up married. I told you to be careful because it would happen again, and you didn't believe me."

She laughed. "I totally forgot about that, but I guess you were right. I'm *really* glad you were right." She thought about all that had happened since the first day she saw Damian on the cruise and realized it had all been leading to this moment. What began as a cruise-ship fling would end in a lifetime of love and happiness. He was everything she could want and more, and she couldn't wait to start their life together.

Over the past year, even with the times apart, she and Damian had grown closer. Karen had settled well into her job as principal, even more so with Nikki gone. As Melissa had predicted, all Nikki's lies and drama had cost her her job. Karen's mind went back to her soon-to-be husband. After much discussion, she and Damian had decided to live in San Jose for at least another year, and then reexamine their options. A knock sounded on the door, and Melissa entered.

"I think it's time," she said with a smile. "Your dad is on his way."

Karen shared one more hug with Janae and Melissa, and they left just as Karen's father entered.

"Ready to go, angel girl?"

"I am, Daddy."

She linked her arm with his, and he escorted her out to where Damian awaited.

Damian paced the length of the floor in the room, waiting for his wedding to start. He didn't remember being this nervous last time.

"You're about to wear a hole in the floor, and I don't think the pastor would be pleased," Kyle teased. "Sit down. You're making me dizzy."

Troy laughed. "What's the problem? You've done this before."

"I know, but not like *this*." He couldn't explain it, but this time felt different.

"Are you having second thoughts?"

"No, nothing like that. I can't wait to make Karen my wife." He stopped. "Are you sure you guys are okay with me working from San Jose?" They had agreed to use Skype for most of their meetings, and Damian would join them at the conference sites, only coming to the North Carolina office when necessary. Troy had insisted on hiring someone part-time to do some of the local workshops to give Damian extra time with Karen. Kyle's younger brother had completed his final tour in the military and agreed to house-sit until Damian and Karen moved back.

"Damian, we've gone over this ten times." Kyle put his hands on Damian's shoulders. "Relax, man. It's all good."

Wiping beads of perspiration off his forehead, he nodded. "I know. I know. Do you have the ring, Troy?"

Troy threw up his hands. "Lord, please let this man hurry up and get married so he can drive someone else crazy."

"I'm not that bad," Damian grumbled.

Kyle and Troy shared a look and said, "Yeah, you are."

The three men burst out laughing and turned at the sound of the door opening.

The minister entered. "Are you ready, son?"

"Definitely," Damian answered.

"That's what I like to hear. Let's go meet your bride."

Damian, Troy and Kyle followed the minister to the sanctuary and the candlelight ceremony began. Janae and Melissa looked beautiful in their dresses, as did the little flower girl—one of Karen's young cousins. The ring bearer, another one of her family members, walked solemnly down the aisle and took his place next to Damian.

He glanced over to the mothers sitting in the front row. Both had tissues and were wiping their eyes. He'd had an opportunity to talk with William and Rhonda Morris and found them to be warm and caring people. Damian assured them he would always love and protect their daughter. They expressed their joy in gaining him as a son, and he felt blessed to have them as in-laws.

The doors opened, and when he saw Karen standing at the back holding her father's arm, he thought his heart would beat out of his chest. Beautiful didn't come close to describing how she looked in the strapless white dress that shimmered with every step. It took everything he had not to rush down the aisle. Kyle must have sensed his urgency because he placed a staying hand on Damian's arm.

"Easy, man."

It seemed to take forever for her to reach him, and when she did, Damian took her hand, brought it to his lips and kissed the back. He mouthed, *I love you*, and turned toward the minister. They repeated their vows, and Monte sang the song he'd sung for Janae on the cruise. Just like the last time, it moved Karen to tears. Throughout it all, he never took his eyes off her. At long last, he heard the words he had been waiting for.

"I now pronounce you husband and wife. Damian, you may kiss your bride."

"Finally," he breathed.

Karen reached up and gently touched his face. "This is the happiest day of my life. I love you very much, Damian."

"And I love you more." He gently wiped away her tears and lowered his head for their first kiss as husband and wife. He tried to convey just how much he loved her in the tender but passionate kiss.

Applause sounded all around them, but he kept right on kissing his wife.

Kyle elbowed him. "All right, that's enough. Save it for tonight."

Reluctantly, he lifted his head. They filed out along with the bridal party, then came back to take pictures. Damian noticed the subtle touches and heated looks Kyle and Melissa were trading and shook his head.

After taking pictures, they got into the back of a limousine waiting to take them to the reception hall.

Damian pulled Karen onto his lap. "So, Mrs. Bradshaw, are you sure you're okay with delaying our honeymoon?" School would resume on Monday, and Damian and Kyle had three scheduled conferences in San Francisco.

"Yes, Mr. Bradshaw. Although I do expect you to make it up to me."

"I know just the thing," he murmured, placing kisses along the column of her neck.

"Oh? And what might that be?"

"A cruise."

"Ooh, that sounds like fun. You owe me two nights anyway."

He chuckled, and their lips met again in a deep, provocative kiss that held the promise of more to come.

That first day, Kyle had said she had *permanent* and *keeper* stamped all over her, and he had been right. Karen was a definite keeper. Damian had been given a second chance, and he intended to love and cherish her for the rest of his life.

* * * * *

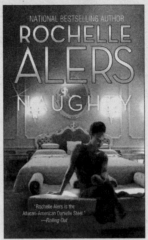

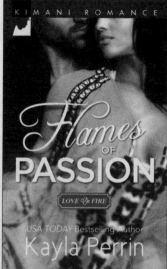

REQUEST YOUR FREE BOOKS!

2 FREE NOVELS PLUS 2 FREE GIFTS!

KIMANI ROMANCE ™

Love's ultimate destination!

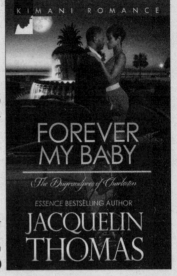